IN THE SCRAPE

IN THE SCRAPE

by

James Newman & Mark Steensland

"Anybody who has survived his childhood has enough information about life to last him the rest of his days."

—Flannery O'Connor

PART ONE

CHAPTER ONE

Six days before our lives were turned upside-down out there in the woods, when we stopped talking about running away and finally did it for real, I lay in bed beside my brother and scolded him for the umpteenth time: "I told you to stop doing that. Sometimes I think they switched babies at the hospital and Mom brought home some psycho's brat instead."

"I'm just kissing her picture," Matthew said. His breath smelled like the Spaghetti-O's we had eaten for dinner. "What's so wrong with that?"

"It's *weird*."

He feigned a hurt expression, but he knew I was only joking. Although I acted as if everything he did irked me to no end, there's not a lot I wouldn't have done back then to make my little brother happy.

By the orange glow of the Wolf Man nightlight plugged into the wall between our beds, we stared at the photo together. Our mother looked so happy in that dog-eared Polaroid. She stood in front of a green car. She wore a blue dress that was stretched tight against her belly (she had been pregnant with Matthew when the picture was taken). Her dark hair was tied up in a tight little bun and her smile was as bright as the sun.

"I miss her so bad, Jake."

"I know," I said. "We all do. I still wish you wouldn't do that."

"Dad does it. He slobbers all over the one on top of the TV."

"When he's drunk," I said. "Are you drunk?"

"Of course not!" Matthew giggled.

I shot a glance through the open doorway, out into the hall, where a bluish light flickered on the wall. I heard the canned laughter of a studio audience, followed by a low cough. A floorboard creaked.

I didn't have to tell him to keep his voice down. He snuggled up closer to me and whispered, "I'm never drinking that stuff. I'd rather eat poop."

"Like I said, you are *so* weird."

I was thirteen years old on the night in question, Matthew had turned nine the week before, and while I didn't fully understand such matters when I was a kid, I remember wishing he would feel that way forever about finding solace at the bottom of a bottle. He didn't turn out exactly like our father, thank God, but there is a lot more of Kurt Bradersen in both of us than I care to admit. A guy can't help what's in his blood.

I sat up on one elbow, took the photo from his hand. As much as we loved looking at it, we never kept it out for very long. This made it feel *sacred,* somehow. Once Matthew started giving it smooches, it was time to put Mom back in the box. Still, I took my turn to stare at it, trying to remember more about her. I was eight the last time I had seen my mother. My memories of her were like trying to view a loved one through eyes wrapped with gauze in the wake of a terrible accident. I couldn't imagine what it was like for poor Matthew.

"Jake, are you crying?"

"Boys don't cry, butthead."

I sniffled, wiped my eyes on the sleeve of my Scooby-Doo pajamas. I was convinced that I had long ago outgrown such silliness, but the PJs were warm and there is a ton of truth to that old cliché *beggars can't be choosers.* The Scooby-Doos had been in a bag of hand-me-downs some local folks had donated to our family the previous Christmas. It could have been worse. I was pretty sure the ones Matthew wore–red with yellow stars all over them–were made for a girl.

I slid Mom's photo back into the shoebox between us. There wasn't much in there besides our beloved Polaroid: some pencils, a notepad, a box of snap'n pops, a miniature Bowie knife in a black canvas sheath, and two old Star Wars figures (an R2-D2 and a headless C-3PO). Mostly the box was a place where we could hide the money we had been saving. It wasn't for shiny new bicycles, the latest remote-control gadget, or trendy tennis shoes endorsed by our favorite athlete. Our secret stash was for something much more important.

Matthew sucked his thumb as he watched me remove the notepad and a pencil from the box. It was a habit of his that I hated, but I never mentioned it. Dad berated him enough about it for the both of us. Matthew would still be sucking his thumb during his first year of middle school; it only went away after he started seeing a therapist.

"Okay," I said. "I got five dollars from Miss Gossett for walking her dog yesterday. Ten for raking the Hoefles' backyard." I scribbled some notes on the pad. "Brings us to a hundred and thirty-five bucks. Which means we've got a week to come up with almost three hundred dollars. Shit…"

"You shouldn't cuss," Matthew said. "It's not Christian."

I ignored him, chewed on the end of my pencil as I thought aloud, "That's just for the bus tickets. Can't see any way around it. We're gonna have to do something drastic."

"*Jacob*. You better not be thinking what I think you're thinking."

"If it's what I think you think I'm thinking, it's our only option. I told you before, squirt, we might not have a choice. We're running out of time."

"But that's *stealing*."

"Grandpa left those books to us."

"He left them to Dad, you mean."

"So he could sell them one day, and we could go to college. I don't even know if I want to go to college."

"But what if he catches us? We'd be in so much trouble."

"Matthew, do you want to go to California to live with Mom or not?"

He nodded.

"Okay, then. Sometimes a man's gotta do what a man's gotta do."

We heard heavy footsteps approaching down the hallway then. I shoved everything back into the box, threw it under the bed. Our heads hit my pillow at the same time. I pulled the covers up, wrapped one arm around Matthew, and lay as still as a corpse a second before Dad's bulk darkened the doorway.

My brother pretended to snore. It wasn't the least bit convincing.

"Matthew, what are you doing in Jake's bed?" Dad said.

"He had a bad dream," I said.

"Didn't ask you."

"I had a bad dream," Matthew said.

Dad took a step into the room. I smelled sweat beneath cheap cologne but no alcohol. Earlier that evening, he had attended a dinner honoring local small-business owners, and he had wanted to impress. Plus, tomorrow was Sunday. The night was still young, however, and our father was never one to worry too much about going to church with a hangover.

"He was scared, Dad," I said. "We knew you got in late. I didn't want him to bother you. It's my fault. Please don't be mad at him?"

Dad said, "In your own bed, Matthew. Now. You're too old for this nonsense."

"Yes, sir." Matthew hurried across the room like someone caught in a tornado, trying to make it to the cellar before the funnel cloud devoured everything in its path. He jumped into his bed.

"And what did I tell you about sucking your thumb? You a little baby?"

"No, sir."

"Then stop it. I'm gonna start busting your butt every time I see that."

"How did it go?" I said.

"How did what go?" Dad said.

"Your dinner?"

"Too high-falutin' for me. If I'd known it was a suit-and-tie affair, I would have skipped it."

Dad left the room, closing the door behind him.

Matthew waited until his footsteps had faded into the distance before he whispered, "Do you really think the books are worth that much?"

"That's what Grandpa said."

"I hope he was right."

"Me too," I said. "If not, I'll figure something out."

"I know you will," he said. "You always do."

CHAPTER TWO

For a little while, when I was around Matthew's age, I wanted to be a famous magician when I grew up. I bought a kit at a thrift shop–it was missing some pieces, including the collapsible top-hat that was an essential part of any illusionist's attire, but I loved it all the same–and I practiced enough to become proficient at some of the simpler tricks. Matthew had been consistently amazed. My friends at school pretended to be impressed. Meanwhile, Dad mentioned at every opportunity that he wished his boys wanted to learn how to do "useful" stuff like hunt and fish and fix cars. To no one's surprise more than my own, however, it was my father who cheered the loudest when I showed off my skills in my fifth-grade talent show. I remember thinking for one incredible evening that he was truly proud of me, but the feeling only lasted until he bought his next case of Pabst Blue Ribbon, and I realized that his enthusiasm was an illusion, just like those silly parlor tricks I performed before several dozen parents, teachers, and students.

As much as I had developed a knack for turning cups of water into confetti and pulling scarves out of my sleeve, there was one magician's skill I was never able to master. I had spent hours in front of my bedroom mirror trying to perfect the art of sleight of hand–palming coins, picking Matthew's pocket without him knowing–but I never got the hang of it. I remember thinking a lot about my brief desire to be the next David Copperfield and how he made it all look so *easy* on the day I tried to lift fifty dollars from the church collection plate.

"Today's offering will now be received," said Pastor Burnside. "May the Lord use our gifts as He sees fit and bless us in return."

I stood, approached the pulpit. I walked with my head held high, as passing around the collection plate was considered a great honor. I could feel the other kids staring at me with what I imagined was murderous envy.

My fellow usher was a farmer whose Sunday best always consisted of wrinkled khakis and a T-shirt sporting the logo of his family business (GRANDDAD'S DAIRY, LLC), as if there was no better place to advertise than in the Lord's house. He had the unlikely surname of Weener, but the hilarity of that had worn off long ago; Matthew and I had learned our lesson the first time Dad heard us snickering about it, after the farmer stood one Sunday and asked the congregation to remember the Weeners in prayer.

We each picked up a collection plate and made our way down the aisle while the pianist played "All Things Come of Thee." My plate filled up quickly–if only because there were more worshippers seated on my side of the sanctuary–and this made me walk with my head held even higher, as if it were some kind of contest between Mr. Weener and me.

About halfway down the aisle, though, as I stopped to pass my plate to the Latham family–Doug, Evette, and their newborn, Dougie Jr.– everything changed.

I didn't plan to do it. Yet the idea came to me the moment I saw Mr. Latham take out his wallet and lay a crisp fifty-dollar bill on top of the smaller bills and pledge envelopes already heaped on my plate. It was as if the Devil himself whispered in my ear: *Take it, Jacob.*

No one was watching me. At least, I didn't think so.

Just take it. Don't do it for yourself. Do it for your brother. You want a better life for him, right? All you have to do is take it.

"Hey, Jake!" Matthew said then, from the next-to-last pew where we sat every Sunday. He waved at me as if I had been gone for years, like the prodigal son in the Bible.

Dad flicked the back of his ear with a middle finger, dropped a handful of coins into my plate as I passed. Matthew winced.

When we were done, Mr. Weener and I were supposed to stand at the rear of the sanctuary until the pianist wrapped up her song, at which point we would return to the front of the church to hand over our bounty to Pastor Burnside.

I glanced over at Mr. Weener. He was staring straight ahead.

I slipped my hand into the pile of money, grabbed a corner of Mr. Latham's fifty-dollar bill, where it lay beneath a rainbow-printed personal check…

…and looked up to see Ms. Anthony glaring at me from across the room.

She was a tall blonde divorcee a few years older than Dad. She wore a white dress with matching gloves, a silver brooch shaped like a cross. On more than one occasion, I had seen my father's eyes linger on her boobs for longer than they should have. Not that I could blame him; at that age I was just beginning to appreciate the female form myself, but while Ms. Anthony was not unattractive, I always thought there was something *mean* about her face, with those piercing blue eyes and her sharp, almost masculine jaw. I suppose it was a look that worked for her, as Ms. Anthony was the principal of a high school on the "bad side of town" (a school that I would one day attend). Only her hot-pink lipstick, a garish shade more suitable for a teenager, belied her professional demeanor.

I smiled at Ms. Anthony. She didn't smile back.

Shit.

My face grew hot. I wondered if I would have to answer for that come Judgment Day. Surely it was a sin to even *think* a curse word in church (ushers, I assumed, were held to an even higher standard).

Then again, it couldn't have been worse than thievery.

I was *so* busted.

Twenty minutes later, we were gathered in the Fellowship Building behind the church, where the congregation convened after the service for coffee, donuts, and chitchat.

"Jacob," Dad said, "you remember Ms. Anthony."

I swallowed a lump in my throat that felt as large as my fist.

"She says you might have something you wanna tell me."

I shrugged. Looked down at my little brother as if he might save me somehow. Matthew ducked behind Dad, as if he also knew about my sin and wished to dodge the lightning bolt that was undoubtedly headed my way.

"Jacob?" Dad said. "Speak up."

"I don't know what you want me to say."

"Mr. Bradersen?" said Ms. Anthony. "May I...?"

Dad stepped back and made a gesture that said: *Be my guest.*

"I saw what you did, young man," said Ms. Anthony, "and you should be ashamed of yourself."

I blinked at her. She blinked back.

"Best you come clean now, Jake," Dad said, "if you don't want things to be a lot harder on you when we get home."

Matthew stepped out from behind him just long enough to chime in, "She told Dad you stole money from God."

"Zip it, Matthew," Dad said. "Nobody's talking to you."

"Yeah," I said. "Zip it, Matthew."

My brother disappeared behind Dad again.

"I'm so disappointed in you, Jacob," said Ms. Anthony.

I chewed on my bottom lip, stared down at my shoes.

"Well?" Dad said. "You gonna talk, or just stand there like a knot on a log?"

"I don't have any idea what she's talking about," I said.

"He's lying," Ms. Anthony said. "I'm sorry, Mr. Bradersen, but, plain as day, I saw Jacob take a bill from the plate and slide it into his pocket."

"Turn out your pockets, son," Dad said.

"You believe her over me? But...she lies all the time!"

Ms. Anthony gasped.

"She puts those little pledge envelopes in the plate. Empty ones. So everybody will think she's giving money to the Lord, but there's really nothing inside of them."

Ms. Anthony held one hand to her bosom. All the color drained from her face. "Why, I never!"

Exactly, I thought. *But everyone* thinks *you do.*

Dad's face burned bright red. He shifted his weight from one foot to the other, glanced back and forth between Ms. Anthony and me. I saw his right hand ball into a fist, but for once I did not recoil. He would never hit me here.

"Why on Earth would you say such a thing?" Ms. Anthony asked me.

"You know it's true. I help count the money sometimes. Your envelope always has pink lipstick on it. And it's empty *every time.*"

"Jesus," Dad hissed under his breath.

This time, when we glared at one another, Ms. Anthony was the first to look away. She whirled around on her heels and *clop-clop-clopp*ed out of the Fellowship Building. I remember thinking it sounded like a horse escaping from its stable.

"Dad," I said. "It's true."

"Turn out your pockets right now. I'm not gonna tell you again."

Matthew peeked out from behind Dad, sucking on his thumb as he watched me obey.

I showed what was in my pockets: nothing but lint and a shiny penny. The penny clattered to the floor, rolled around. When I didn't pick it up, Matthew claimed it for himself.

"Can we go home now?" I said.

Dad looked around the room, at several members of the congregation who had witnessed the debacle. As he met their gaze, they quickly turned away, either finding something interesting to talk about among themselves or deciding it was time to grab another donut.

"Get in the truck," Dad said through clenched teeth. "I don't want to hear another word from either of you."

CHAPTER THREE

We owned a 1972 International pickup that ran about half the time, mostly thanks to the power of prayer. Its engine sounded like an old man dying of emphysema. I never understood that, since Dad was a mechanic by trade. The truck was the color of dried blood. It had a large crack in the passenger-side window (the one time I asked him how it got there, Dad grunted something about shutting up a man who asked too many questions).

The vehicle was equipped with an old three-on-the-tree clutch. My father worked those controls as if it came no less natural to him than breathing. On more than one occasion as I watched him drive, I was reminded of Han Solo maneuvering the Millennium Falcon through hyperspace. He always drove too fast down the curvy backroads of our hometown, but he never got a speeding ticket (probably because he had been friends with our former sheriff and used to service the department's vehicles). Truth told, Matthew and I loved it, even as we held on for dear life…as long as we knew he hadn't been drinking.

On the day in question, though, I wished he would ease off the gas. Sweat trickled down my temples as we pulled onto Rickman Road about a mile-and-a-half from home. I imagined opening the door, throwing myself from the truck to avoid what was coming. Most children are afraid of the boogeyman in the basement or monsters under their bed. There was nothing that frightened me more than my own father when he was angry. After the confrontation at church, I assumed I wouldn't be able to sit down for days, that Dad's wrath would leave me with welts on my bottom and bruises on the backs of my legs.

But that wasn't what happened.

We were almost home before he said anything. When he finally spoke, his tone wasn't angry. It was that of a man who has been beaten down and doesn't know how much more he can take.

"I've never been so embarrassed in my life," he said.

"I'm sorry," I said. "I don't know why she would–"

He surprised me with a deep chuckle. "Gotta admit, I almost cracked up when you said what you said. The look on her face! She always did think she was better than us. Like I'm not good enough to support my family, my kid's gotta steal like some welfare nigger?"

I gazed out at the woods through the cracked window. Two young men with long hair walked along the side of the road, carrying BB guns. One of them flicked a cigarette onto the pavement as we passed.

"Still," he said, "you gotta respect your elders, son."

"Yes, sir," I said.

We pulled into our muddy driveway, the truck's shocks squeaking and groaning. Dad opened his door before we came to a complete stop, as if the beer in our fridge was a magnet and he was a man made of metal. He would spend the rest of his afternoon in front of the TV, drinking and watching M*A*S*H reruns.

"Dad," said Matthew, "can me and Jake go to the park?"

Dad thought about it for a moment. "Change outta your good clothes. Eat lunch. Then you can go."

"Cool," said Matthew. "You wanna, Jake? Wanna go to the park?"

"I sorta had plans already," I said.

"What plans?" Dad scoffed at me as he unlocked the front door. I noticed his hands were shaking. "Thirteen years old, you might think you're all grown-up, but you got a long way to go. You don't make 'plans' without clearing it with your father first."

"I wanted to see if I could walk Miss Gossett's dog again," I said.

"Why?"

"Thought I'd save up a few dollars to help out with Christmas this year."

His brow furrowed, as if he was trying to peer into my brain to figure out if I was telling him the truth. Of course, come Christmastime I planned to be two thousand miles away.

He shoved through the door. "Leave that old woman alone. It won't kill you to spend some time with your brother. Besides, you know we ain't supposed to work on the Sabbath."

Matthew beamed at me. I shot him a dirty look. But I didn't really mind. I enjoyed spending time with my brother, and, after what happened at church, Dad could have used his belt on me instead of his hateful tongue.

"Home before dark, right?" Dad stood in our bedroom doorway, one hand scratching at an itchy spot on top of his head, the other wrapped around a can of Pabst Blue Ribbon. He had already changed out of his Sunday best into a pair of gray sweatpants and an old Kenny Rogers tank top.

"Dang it, Matthew," I said. "If you want me to do this, stay still."

I knelt before my him, tying his shoes while he sat on the edge of his bed. Not only was my brother still sucking his thumb at nine years old, he hadn't yet mastered how to tie his own shoes. Something about that made me despise our father even more.

"And stay away from the creek," Dad said. "I told you what kinda stuff goes on down there."

"We won't go near the creek," I said.

Dad had seen a report on the local news earlier that year about some folks who had been picking up trash in the woods near our favorite park. Along with the plastic grocery bags and fast-food wrappers strewn about the area, the clean-up crew had discovered two syringes floating in the creek. While the culprit could have been a litterbug with diabetes, thanks to sensationalistic journalism my father–along with most of our hometown–was convinced that hypodermic needles regularly coated the creek's surface like algae, and if good kids ventured too close to the dirty water they were sure to end up with AIDS, an addiction to heroin, or both.

I wondered how hard he would search for us if something bad did ever happen to Matthew and me. What would he do six days from now, when we were suddenly gone? I imagined our neighbors combing through the weeds on either side of Crites Road, shouting our names until they were hoarse…scuba divers scouring the rocky bottom of the creek, hoping they would find nothing but tadpoles and turtles…while Dad sat at home, snoring in front of the TV, a can of beer nestled in his crotch.

But that was stupid. Of course he would care. He could be a real bastard sometimes, but it would destroy him when we went missing. He would probably drink himself to death.

That thought brought an evil grin to my face.

"What's so funny, Jake?" Matthew asked me.

I finished tying his shoe, gave his knee a playful squeeze. "Nothing, squirt. Let's go."

"You make sure you keep an eye on your brother," Dad said.

"Of course."

"Home before dark," he said again, stifling a belch before he turned to leave the room.

When we were outside, Matthew headed straight for the storage shed at the rear of our property. It was a rust-speckled aluminum building that sat beside a weed-choked dog lot (Dad once owned a pit bull that he loved more than anything on Earth, but the dog got spooked one 4th of July, dug out under its fence, and we never saw it again). The shed was cluttered with all of the junk our family had collected through the years: an old drill press Dad didn't use anymore, boxes of old clothes, a bicycle I used to adore before Dad ran over it the previous summer, and a sofa he had muscled out into the yard one night and set on fire (it was the only time I ever called the police during one of his tirades, because I was terrified he was going to burn everything to the ground if someone didn't stop him)— not to mention a pile of Mom's possessions she had left behind. I never liked going in there, and I avoided it if possible. Not because of the stench of burned sofa that still permeated the shed three years after Dad doused the thing with kerosene and struck a match. It was because I hated seeing Mom's stuff shoved into that cobwebby corner like a filthy secret. I didn't like thinking about how, if she was coming back for her belongings, she would have done so by now. And that filled me with doubts about my master plan. In those days, hope was all we had, my little brother and me. Hope and a little money we had saved inside a shoebox.

Matthew tried to lift the door, but it was stuck.

"What in the world are you doing?" I asked him.

"I wanna take Big Red."

I gave an exaggerated sigh, as if this would delay us by two or three hours. "Can't we just *go?*"

"Pleeeeease?"

Another sigh. I yanked up the door, held it open for him about three feet off the ground. He ducked under it. There was an autumn chill in the air, but the afternoon sun was warm on my shoulders. I smelled dust, mildew, and, as always, burnt sofa. I sneezed. A minute or so later, my brother came out carrying Big Red. He had cherished that giant plastic ball ever since Mom bought it for him when he was so small he could barely lift it. The only reason he didn't keep it in the house was because Dad couldn't stand the sight of it and had once threatened to pop it with his pocketknife if it kept getting in his way. Big Red was like a crimson cape waved in front of a pissed-off bull, as far as Dad was concerned, though I suspected the main reason he despised it was because it was one more thing that reminded him of Mom.

I dropped the door, and we headed through the woods toward the park.

We stepped out of the woods onto a strip of land consumed by tall brown weeds. Only a set of railroad tracks and a small brick building–formerly the offices of PHYLLIS MARKLAND, D.D.S., according to the sign out front–sat between us and the park. The dentist had closed up shop long ago. The lot was empty except for a hungry-looking cat. It scampered away at the sight of us, ignoring Matthew's *here, kitty-kitty…*

Up ahead sat the old city park. Beyond it, over the crest of a grassy hill, was Crites Road, which led into town. To our left, two basketball goals stood over a patch of cracked concrete, like tired old sentinels guarding something that no one would ever want to steal. The playground consisted of little more than some monkey bars and a crooked swing-set. Past the playground sat a drinking fountain and a small brick building, which was where the restrooms were located. Beyond that was a tall chain-link fence.

"Last one to the water fountain is a rotten egg!" I said.

Matthew took off before I could call *ready-set-go*.

"You sneaky little shit!" I hollered after him, as if we hadn't played this game a thousand times before.

Although I never believed the rumors about gangs of wild-eyed delinquents roaming the park in search of younger kids to lure into their world of drug-induced madness, I was old enough to recognize that there was something a tad unsavory about this place. It was as if the new city park that had opened the previous summer on the opposite side of town had leached all life from this one, like a vampire growing more vivacious as his victim wastes away into nothing. Over there, the picnic tables didn't have racist epithets carved into them or bubblegum stuck underneath like clusters of alien tumors. The basketball goals had clean white nets and bright yellow lines on their newly-blacktopped courts. Over there, the local Jaycees hosted events like the Family Fireworks Extravaganza and the Annual Easter Egg Hunt for kids whose mothers hadn't run off to California.

The rest of our town had forgotten this place. But Matthew and I loved the old park because it was *ours*.

Matthew kicked Big Red ahead of him as he ran, which slowed him down but not by much. Soccer was his favorite sport, and I had little doubt that my brother would have exceled in it if given the opportunity. Unfortunately, when he had brought a flyer home from school one day informing parents that it was time to sign their kids up for a county team, Dad threw it in the trash. He claimed we couldn't afford it, asked Matthew if he was a Mexican 'cause only spics liked soccer.

"Congrats," I said when the race was over.

"You let me win."

"Not true." I bent over, hands on my knees, pretending to catch my breath. "You must have hit a wormhole or something, jumped through space and time like Doctor Who."

"What's a doctorhoo?"

I had never seen the show myself. I had only heard about it from kids at school, friends who could afford cable TV and shared with me all the awesome shows you could find on there.

"Forget it," I said. "I gotta whizz."

"I'll wait here."

I jogged off toward the restrooms, heard him fussing with the button on the water fountain. Like he didn't know by now that it hadn't worked since the pipes froze the previous winter.

I locked the stall door. Ignored the graffiti scratched into the yellow paint all around me: MANDY SENK WILL BLOW ANYBODY...AC/DC RULES...PRINCIPAL HARWOOD EATS POOP (that last one was my own contribution, scrawled there a lifetime ago when I was still in elementary school). I flushed the toilet, since whomever had used the stall before me hadn't been courteous enough to do so. I did it only to breathe a little easier; despite what I had told Matthew, I didn't have to whizz.

I unzipped my jeans, reached into the front of my underwear. Pulled out the grape-sized wad of paper that was tucked beneath my scrotum. I grinned as I unfolded it, turning the misshapen ball into a wrinkled green rectangle.

I admired the fifty-dollar bill for a minute or more. Turned it over and over in my hands, studying Grant's face on one side and the Capitol building on the other. The bearded President's stern expression scolded me: *little scoundrel, you should be ashamed of yourself.*

"Yeah, that's what they all say. But you're dead. Who are you gonna tell?"

I chuckled, stuffed the bill into my back pocket, then hurried out of the restroom.

My mood turned dark as soon as I stepped outside.

Matthew sat on the ground next to the water fountain, his head in his hands. He was crying.

"Matthew? What's wrong?"

He didn't look up. He slowly raised one finger to point at something behind me.

I felt sick, knew what I would see before I even turned around.

CHAPTER FOUR

Their leader's name was Caleb Caldwell. He had decided from the moment we met in the third grade that his goal in life was to torment me at every opportunity. Thanks to Caleb, I had suffered countless spitballs to the back of my neck, books knocked out of my hands, nicknames so stupid they never caught on with our classmates ("GAYcob BraderSHIT" was his latest and greatest), and brutal punches to the arm that left me sore and purple for days. Caleb was a year older than me, a foot taller, and thirty pounds heavier. He smelled like old sweat-socks. He always wore a red NC State baseball cap, baggy jeans that he was constantly pulling up by one belt loop, and black heavy metal T-shirts (his favorite band in the world: AC/DC). He had a bushy unibrow and a wide, ape-like nose.

His buddies were Zack Gorman, a tall blonde boy who would eventually go on to be a local basketball star once he stopped hanging around folks like Caleb, and Austin Hipps, a fat redhead with more freckles on his face and arms than I have ever seen on one person.

"Want your faggot ball back?" said Caleb. "Why don't you come and get it, crybaby?"

Austin had his arms wrapped around Big Red as if he were manhandling a hostage. The chain-link fence rattled against their backs.

"Come on, Caleb," I groaned. "Why don't you just leave us alone?"

"Consider it payback," Caleb said. "For sending your dad to my house. A real man takes care of his own fights."

A week earlier, my father had driven to the trailer park across town where Caleb's family lived, he had dragged Bob Caldwell out into his front yard while his neighbors looked on, and he had threatened to stomp a mudhole in the smaller man's ass if he didn't do something about his good-for-nothing son. Dad had been fuming over the fact that Caleb had busted my nose the day before. It wasn't my injury that enraged him, of course; it was because I had been wearing his old Army jacket during the scuffle and now it was ruined with permanent bloodstains.

Big Red squeaked in Austin's grip, as if crying out for help.

"Whatcha think we should do with it?" Caleb asked his pals.

"We should piss on it," said Austin.

"Or shit on it," said Zack.

"Nah, I got a better idea…"

Caleb snatched the ball from Austin's hands and threw it over the fence.

"No!" Matthew screamed.

The bullies high-fived each other. Their laughter echoed through the park.

I trembled with rage. I wanted nothing more than to leap upon Caleb and tear him to pieces. But I knew he would have pounded me into the ground with little effort. And where would that leave my brother?

In the distance, I watched a lime-green Public Transit bus stop near the entrance of the park. An old man in a newsboy cap stepped off and hobbled down the sidewalk with the help of a cane. I wondered if there was anyone on the bus who could help us. But then it pulled away from the curb and continued along Crites Road, transporting its oblivious passengers to their perfect, bully-free lives.

"Come on, Matthew."

I ran for the fence, scaled it in record time. The whole thing wobbled, felt like it might collapse beneath me, but held. I straddled the rusty top rail, waiting for Matthew.

Caleb and his crew gawked at me like I was crazy.

Matthew said, "But Jake…Dad said we were supposed to stay out of the creek!"

"You want your ball back, don't you?"

He nodded. Sniffled.

I held a hand out toward him. "Come on then, squirt."

Matthew sprinted past the bullies, called them big, ugly buttholes.

Caleb told him to watch his mouth unless he wanted to go swimming with his faggot ball. Zack said I would be too chickenshit to stop it. Austin squeezed his crotch with one freckled hand, told us to lick these balls.

I helped Matthew over the fence, and their hateful laughter faded in the distance as we set out to rescue Big Red.

A steep hill carpeted with fallen leaves and pine needles led down to the creek bank. There was something dead close by—I could smell an odor of decay in the air.

"You just *had* to bring your stupid ball, didn't you?"

I spotted Big Red on the other side of the creek. The ball was stuck between two large rocks. There was no way I could reach it without going into the water. Unless…

A massive oak had fallen across the creek. Its trunk hung at an angle about three feet above the water.

I ordered Matthew not to follow me before climbing on. Carefully, I worked my way along the makeshift bridge like a circus performer on a tightrope. Somewhere near the middle, I spotted the source of that sickly-sweet stench of something rotting. A leafy squirrel's nest had been built in the branches of the oak. The nest and its inhabitants now lay flattened beneath it on the opposite side of the creek.

"Jacob," Matthew said, "please be careful…"

"You just keep watch and make sure those jerks don't come back for more."

"Got it." He crossed his arms in front of his skinny chest and turned to face the fence as if he had been given the most important job in the history of the universe.

And then I fell in.

The water barely came up to my thighs. But it was *cold*. I knew it was ridiculous, but for a second I thought about junkies' needles jutting up from the creek bed like tiny punji sticks waiting to infect my ankles with AIDS.

"Dammit!"

Matthew giggled.

"If I didn't love you so much, I'd hate you right now," I said, as I waded through the water and grabbed Big Red.

I made my way back to solid ground.

Matthew stopped laughing. He eyed my dripping clothes with a horrified expression. "You are gonna be in so much trouble, Jake."

"Probably. And it's all your fault."

I tossed the ball his way, then we headed for home.

"Maybe he won't notice," Matthew said, as I lifted the door of the storage shed so he could put the ball away. "You could run inside and change while I create a...dieservance?"

"Diversion." I shook my head. "This is Dad we're talking about. The mood he's in today, he could be drunk off his ass and he'd notice a penny missing from his change jar."

"I guess you're right."

We walked toward the house. "I know I'm right. Oh, and don't say anything about what happened with Caleb. We've got enough problems with those guys already."

"Don't worry," said Matthew. "I promise I won't say nothing about that."

"You promise you won't say nothin' about what?"

My breath caught in my throat. My heart skipped a beat. I froze mid-step, and Matthew crashed into me from behind.

Dad sat behind the wheel of his pickup. The driver-side door hung open. The engine wasn't running, but I could hear Loretta Lynn singing "Stand By Your Man" on the truck's piece-of-crap stereo.

He lifted a can of beer to his mouth, slurped at it loudly. "You boys get over here. I wanna talk to you."

We did as we were told.

He looked me up and down. "You're soaking-wet. Been in the creek, I'm guessing. Even though I told you not to be messing around down there."

"No," I said, desperately trying to conjure up a lie he would believe.

"You wasn't in the creek?"

"No, sir."

Dad tipped back the can, guzzled what was left inside. Crumpled it up and tossed it onto the seat beside him. "Let's hear it then, Jake. I'm waiting. Wanna hear how dumb you think I am."

"I...we were–"

Matthew tried to save me. His words came out in a desperate jumble: "It was the water fountain! Jake tried to get a drink and it sprayed all over him! You should have seen it, Dad! It was funny."

"*It was funny*," Dad mocked him.

"He looked like a wet dog," Matthew said.

Dad sat there staring at us for what felt like forever, not saying anything, and there was something so *mean* in his eyes, as if my brother and I were the cause of everything that had gone wrong in his life. It was times like these, I remember, when I was most afraid of my father. Not when he was yelling and cursing. He was scariest when he was silent.

In the woods behind our house, a crow cawed.

Dad belched. Killed the ignition. Fumbled with his door handle.

"Get your butts in the house. Fetch my belt from the closet. You know what lying gets you."

Fetching the belt for your own spanking made the whole thing more humiliating. Like a man on death row wiring his own electric chair, or a Salem spinster chopping the wood for her own public funeral pyre. Back then, I often wondered if my father got some sadistic thrill out of it. These days I have no doubt.

Matthew tugged frantically at my shirttail. *Do something...*

"But Dad," I said, "we're not lying!"

"You are." He climbed out of the truck, stepped toward us on unsteady legs. "And you're both gonna learn what it feels like to not sit down for a month." He stuck his finger in my face. "Unless you wanna admit this was all *your* idea? You ought to know better, Jacob. Your brother looks up to you. Admit you been teaching Matthew your bad habits, teaching your brother to *lie,* and we can double up on your whooping. Choice is yours."

"Okay," I said. "I fell in the creek."

"That's what I thought."

"But the wind blew my ball over the fence," Matthew said. "Jake went to get it back. He went to get the ball back for *me*, Daddy!"

Something about my little brother reverting to that word, *Daddy*–an affectionate word neither of us had used for several years–broke my heart worse than anything else.

"More lies," Dad said. "I've heard enough. Get to your room, Matthew, and don't come out 'til I tell you to. Jake, you know the drill."

We ran inside. As I went into Dad's room to get the belt, I prayed it would be over quickly. Sometimes when he was *really* drunk, he got sloppy. Once, he toppled over mid-swing and passed out before my punishment was complete. He was snoring before I got my pants pulled up, and he remembered none of it the next day.

That didn't happen this time.

It was a size 42 faux-leather Walmart special with a giant brass buckle that read "I'D RATHER BE HUNTING", a birthday gift from my mother not long before she left us. I couldn't remember the last time I had seen him wear it. I wondered how she would feel about the fact that he used the belt to beat her children more than he used it to hold up his pants.

It happened the same way every time. Like a ritual. When Dad decided you deserved a spanking, you were to go into the utility room at the rear of the house. You were to lay his belt atop the washer, pull down your pants, then lean against the dryer, a hand gripping each side of the machine as he taught you the error of your ways.

A framed embroidery sampler hung on the wall of the utility room. "THE LOVE OF A FAMILY IS LIFE'S GREATEST BLESSING" it read, inside a border of hearts and flowers. Mom made it when she was pregnant with me. I always stared at it while he was hitting me with the belt, and I assumed Matthew did too.

On the evening in question, I took my punishment like a man. I didn't even cry. I refused to give him the satisfaction.

When he was finished with me, he was red-faced and out of breath. He said, "Now send in your brother. It's his turn."

"What? But you said only me!"

"I *lied*," he said. "How's that feel?"

"I hate you," I said as I pulled up my jeans.

"That's fine," Dad said. "You can hate me all you want. But you only hate me 'cause you don't understand. You don't understand how hard it is to raise two ungrateful brats all by myself. I bust my ass to make sure you two don't want for nothing. All I get in return is a bunch of *lies* every time I turn arou–"

"You're the one who doesn't understand," I said. "But you will. When we're gone."

"Not this again, Jacob." He laughed cruelly. "How many times do I have to say it? *Your mother doesn't want anything to do with you.* That's why she left. She decided she didn't want to be a momma no more. Which means you're stuck with me. I'm all you boys got, whether you like it or not."

"She left because of *you*," I said.

"How come she never calls you on your birthday? Has she ever sent either one of you a Christmas present? No. You know why? Bet you anything it's 'cause she's got a whole new family out there in California, one she likes just fine."

"That's not true!"

"Deep down inside, you know it is. That's the thing about lying, though. You start doubting everything around you, can't tell the difference between what's real and what's not. It all blurs together. Sooner or later, everybody gets hurt."

I glared at him, tried like hell to convince myself that he was wrong about everything.

He gripped his belt tighter. I heard the leather squeak in his hand. "I gotta tell you again to fetch your brother, he's gonna get it twice as bad."

Now I did start crying. "This isn't fair!"

"No," Dad said, "it's not. But that's life, Jacob. Life ain't fair."

It ended with him lurching into our bedroom, grabbing Matthew by the arm, and dragging him from the room as we both pleaded with him to *stop Daddy, please stop, please Daddy, don't do this...*

But he didn't stop for a long time. It went on and on.

I covered my head with my pillow as Matthew's screams filled the house, along with the violent *thwap!* of belt on skin.

I heard them talking for a long while afterward. Muffled voices through the wall. They did that a lot. As if everything was forgiven, and they were suddenly best buddies once Dad was done beating the shit out of him. It used to make me so angry. As if my brother was betraying me. I never asked Matthew what they had discussed, because I wasn't sure I wanted to know.

I prayed he didn't tell Dad what we were planning to do. *Please, God, as long as he doesn't do that...*

Finally, they came back to the bedroom. I noticed they were holding hands. Matthew sniffled softly, but he was no longer crying.

"I want both of you in your pajamas," Dad said. "In bed by eight-thirty. You got school tomorrow."

I heard my belly growl. "What about supper?"

"What about it?" He turned and stomped off down the hall.

Matthew collapsed on his bed, started sucking his thumb.

"Hey, squirt," I whispered. "You okay?"

He didn't reply.

"You hungry?"

He nodded.

"I've got something for you. Tastes better than your thumb, I promise."

He sat up, curious.

I pulled two apples out from under my pillow. Tossed one onto his bed.

"That's not all."

I threw a granola bar at him. It bounced off the wall and into his lap. Its BEST BY date had expired over a month ago, but he didn't have to know that. He offered me a weak smile, tore open the wrapper. I helped myself to the second bar stashed beneath my pillow.

"Where did you get this stuff?" he asked me.

"From the kitchen, where else? Took it while Dad was busy with you."

"You snuck it without asking?"

"We gotta eat, don't we?"

I pulled the shoebox out from under my bed then. Slid the fifty-dollar bill from my back pocket and added it to our stash.

Matthew's jaw dropped, showing me a tongue covered in chunks of chewed-up granola bar.

"We're getting there," I mumbled, talking to myself more than Matthew. "Running out of time, though. If we *have* to take the comics, we'd have plenty left over. Maybe we could buy something nice for Mom and *really* surprise her…"

Funny how, the more I did it, breaking the rules got so much easier. Not to mention it was a tad intoxicating. At this rate, I wondered if I would be robbing liquor stores and smoking the pot by the time I turned sixteen.

Matthew gasped. "So, Ms. Anthony was right? You *did* steal from the collection plate?"

I shrugged. Shoved the shoebox back under the bed. Went to the dresser and pulled out our nightclothes.

"But, Jacob…that's like stealing from God." He gawked at me as he dressed for bed, like he was sure the floor would open up at any moment and the Devil would drag me down to Hell.

"I don't see it that way," I said.

He was unconvinced.

"Look," I said. "If we took the money and spent it on candy or toys? That'd be different. We're doing this because we *have* to."

"It still don't feel right," Matthew said.

"Trust me," I said. "God understands. And if I'm wrong, you don't have to sweat it. *I'm* the one He'll punish."

Matthew dropped the subject for now. I knew we were thinking the same thing, though: *That's not the way it works with Dad. How do we know the Lord is any different?*

CHAPTER FIVE

The sky is the color of concrete…gray as far as the eye can see, like the walls of a maximum-security prison or, worse yet, summer school. It is a sky that holds the threat of rain, maybe even the first snow of the season. The air is cold. The trees are bare and black, like the silhouettes of skeletal hands reaching toward the heavens. Fog swirls about on the forest floor, like ghosts gathered here to conspire about things only the dead can know.

Everything is silent.

But suddenly…a flash of white! Something moves through the foliage. Something BIG. Hoofbeats, like the heart of a sprinter…

It's an albino buck. Out of every thirty-thousand deer born on Earth, only one will be a true albino. He's a gorgeous creature, solid white with haunting eyes of pink. His twelve-point antlers are rubbed clean of velvet, which can only mean one thing: it's rutting season.

The buck scans the woods, searching for any sign of danger…

At a rub, he sniffs the broken bark. He lowers his head and with his mighty rack he peels off more, to make sure his tag is clear. He chews the tips of a low-hanging branch, marking it with the scent of his saliva.

He steps back and paws at the ground, turning over the dead leaves and pine needles to get to the black soil beneath.

He urinates. It runs down his legs, steams in the early morning air as it puddles into the scrape. Later, he will return to this spot to mate with the doe that answers his call…

A twig snaps.

His tail perks up. His nostrils flare.

I peek around a tree, aim my rifle at the buck…but then I hesitate.

"What the hell are you waiting for?"

I glance back at Dad. His face is cloaked in shadow.

"Remember how I showed you. Squeeze the trigger, don't pull it. You got him right where you want him."

I nod, adjust my grip on the gun. It's a bolt-action .257 Winchester Model 70 that once belonged to my grandfather. Now it is mine.

"*Take the shot, Jake. Do it now or he's gonna get away.*"

I chamber a round. The CLACK! of the bolt is deafening. I expect the buck to take off into the woods, but he doesn't. The creature snorts, his breath pluming like smoke into the November air, and he holds his position defiantly.

"*Take the shot,*" *Dad whispers in my ear again.*

"*Okay…*"

I spin around and point the gun at him.

"*Jesus Christ, Jake, what are y–*"

I pull the trigger. His chest explodes. He falls backward into the dirt.

I lower the gun, breathe in the forest air.

At last, we are free. *I can't wait to tell Matthew.*

I look back toward the buck. He's still there. Not moving. Not even blinking. Watching me. But not judging me.

"*Go,*" *I tell him.* "*Run away while you still c–*"

A heavy hand falls on my shoulder.

I turn.

It's Dad. He's alive, doesn't have a mark on him.

He hitches up his orange hunting vest, removes his belt. It slithers through the loops of his britches with a snake-like hissing sound.

"*You disrespectful little shit. You're grounded 'til you're thirty, you hear me? And wait 'til you see what I'm gonna do to your brother. Hope it was worth it…'cause you've only got yourself to blame for what's about to happen.*"

I awoke with a high-pitched shriek. I thrashed about under the covers, dripping with sweat.

Big, work-calloused hands gripped my shoulders.

"Shh. Easy, boy. Easy! You're gonna wake up your brother."

"D-Dad?"

"Whatever you was dreamin' about, it must've been a doozy."

I sat up.

"You okay?"

"Y-Yeah," I said. "I think so."

"See what I mean? This is why you're not allowed to watch those scary movies."

My father and I had fallen asleep in front of the television one Saturday night not too long ago. He awoke at four in the morning to find me sitting wide-eyed in the middle of the living room floor, gnawing at my nails while I watched a heavily-edited version of *The Shining*. He insisted such nonsense would give me nightmares. I suppose my dream about snow-white stags and patricide proved his point. However, the elements of that film which unsettled me the most weren't the malevolent ghosts roaming the corridors of a creepy hotel, but the father who tried to slaughter his family.

"Wanna talk about it?" Dad said. "Sometimes it helps to get it out."

"I was dreaming about hunting the buck."

"You don't say. The albino, you mean?"

I nodded.

He smiled, squeezed my knee with one hand. His breath smelled like onions. "You know…the Iroquois believed dreams were messages straight from the Man Upstairs. Thought they had to do whatever their dreams told them to do, or else."

"Messages from God?" My brain was still foggy, his words only half-making-sense.

"What do you think about that?"

I knuckled grainy sleep-stuff from my eyes, shrugged.

"Did you get him?" he asked.

"What?"

"Said you were dreaming about hunting the buck. Did you get him?"

"Um…yeah. I got him."

"Well, there you go. It's a sign. Maybe the redskins were right. That'd be something, wouldn't it? You bagging that sumbitch on your first trip out?"

"That would be really cool," I said.

For a minute or more he just sat there without saying anything, a dark figure looming over me in the night. My brother snored softly on the other side of the room, one of his nostrils whistling every few seconds.

This time, when his hand squeezed my knee, it wasn't a loving gesture. He did it hard enough to hurt a little bit. When he spoke again his tone had grown colder, "Know what else would be 'cool'?"

"Huh?"

"If you never lie to me again. Nothing burns me up more than when you boys lie to me. I'm scared of what I might do, Jake, if I get that mad again."

You're not the only one, I thought. *It's why, in less than a week, you won't ever see us again...*

"Yes, sir," I said.

"Lemme hear you say it. That's the last time you'll lie to me."

"That's the last time I'll lie to you," I said.

"Good." His hand fell away from my knee. "That's good." He stood. "Now strip these sheets. You pissed the bed. I'd expect such a thing from Matthew, but...my God, Jake, you're almost fourteen years old."

He was right. The ammonia smell hit me now, and I felt the dampness beneath me. I hadn't even realized it before he mentioned it.

I rolled out of bed, started piling the blankets on the floor. "Sorry. I'm sorry. I'll take care of it, Dad."

"See that you do," he said. "I'm going back to bed. Love you, son."

"I love you too," I lied.

CHAPTER SIX

The following afternoon we sat in the front office of my school, waiting for Dad to arrive. The last bell rang at three o' clock. It was a quarter past four and there was still no sign of him.

A few feet away, the janitor, Mr. Odell, pushed a mop around with a bored expression on his face. I stared through the window that looked out onto the campus, watching two boys whose names I didn't know lower the flag on its pole. Behind them, Coach Winfield gathered up some traffic cones in the parking lot with the help of a kid named Bradley Tonkin. Everyone in school thought Buck-Toothed Bradley was the biggest butt-kisser on the face of the Earth. He was the only one who suffered Caleb Caldwell's wrath more than I did, and I suppose that made us friends in a way. Though, I admit, I only talked to him when no one else was around.

I sighed.

On the other side of the room, Mrs. Garrett sighed too.

"Hopefully he'll be here soon," I said.

"Hopefully," said the secretary. She was a chubby dark-haired woman whose daughter, Charlene, sat beside me in Science class.

I slapped my brother lightly on the leg when I saw Dad's truck pull up outside. Matthew had been drawing little piles of poop with flies buzzing around them in his notebook. He finished his latest masterpiece before jumping to his feet.

We watched Dad get out of the truck. He wore blue coveralls and work boots. One of his boots was untied, I noticed. There was a smear of something black across his forehead.

He pushed a button by the door and Mrs. Garrett buzzed him in.

Mr. Odell stepped back to let Dad pass. The janitor mumbled something about the floor being wet. Dad ignored him, ruffled my hair as if everything was A-OK and we hadn't been sitting there waiting on him for almost an hour-and-a-half.

"Sorry," he said to the secretary. "Busy day at the shop. I tend to lose track of time when I'm under the hood."

Mrs. Garrett handed him a pen and a clipboard. "You'll have to sign them out. Just so you know, sir, we're not a daycare. And remember, the little guy attends the elementary school on the other side of the street. He has to cross a four-lane highway to wait here with his brother."

"Looks like he made it okay," Dad said, scribbling his name. "By the way, you can go ahead and mark 'em absent next Monday. It's opening weekend of deer season." He winked at me over his shoulder. "Gonna be Jake's first time, and he can't wait."

Mrs. Garrett didn't say anything, just pursed her lips in disapproval.

Once we were in the truck, Dad said, "Who the hell does she think she is?"

"Mrs. Garrett," I said.

"It was a rhetorical question, Jake. I don't give a damn what her name is. Just another stuck-up cooze, thinks she's better than me." He rolled down his window, hawked up a loogie, and spat it onto the asphalt as he started up the truck. "I was thinking Ford's for dinner. That sound okay with you two?"

"Yayyy!" said Matthew. "My fave!"

"Thought you might like that. Hope you boys are hungry. I could eat a skunk's butthole."

Matthew giggled. I laughed too, couldn't help it.

We headed toward town.

Ford's was an old-fashioned drive-in, all hot-white fluorescent lights and green neon. Matthew wasn't the only one who adored the place. A trip to Ford's was like travelling back in time to a simpler, more innocent era. They played songs by the Coasters, Chuck Berry, and Bill Haley and the Comets on the overhead P.A. system, and the short-skirted waitresses rolled around the lot on roller skates. Dad liked to tell us when he was in a good mood that he had met our mother at Ford's. He claimed she rolled up to his window with his order in hand and he had asked her to be his girlfriend on the spot. I wondered what it was that made her want to be with my father. If he had possessed qualities that made him handsome and good when he was a younger man.

He pulled into one of the parking spots and pushed the little button under the menu ("I wanna do it!" Matthew begged, but Dad ignored him). With his other hand, he scratched furiously at his stubbled chin.

"Welcome to Ford's," said a girl's voice on the speaker. "May I take your order, please?"

Dad told her to make it three cheeseburgers with everything, three orders of curly fries, and three small Cokes.

"I don't want tomato on mine," said Matthew.

"Will that be all, sir?" said the girl on the speaker.

"No tomatoes," Matthew said.

My brother always had this weird hang-up about tomatoes. He said the seeds gave him the creeps. To this day, I have never understood it.

Dad glanced over his shoulder at Matthew. "What's wrong with you? I told you before, it's no good without tomatoes."

"I just don't like 'em," said Matthew.

"He never has," I said.

"Well, he can pick 'em off," said Dad.

I don't know why I continued to argue with him. I suppose it was because I knew I wouldn't have to deal with Dad at all in a few more days. It gave me more courage than I would have possessed otherwise. I couldn't help myself. "Yeah, but…if you tell them no tomatoes, he won't *have* to pick 'em off. Wouldn't that be easier?"

"I already put the order in," said Dad.

Matthew mumbled something about how it wasn't a big deal. Dad glared at me for a minute, looked back at the speaker with an expression that suggested the battered piece of metal had called him something obscene.

"Ya know what?" he snapped at it. "Forget it. Just cancel the whole damn thing."

"I'm sorry?" said the speaker. "What was that?"

"I said, forget it!"

"Are you kidding?" I said.

The tires squealed as Dad reversed and sped out of the lot. In my side mirror, I saw him nearly flatten a young lady skating by with a tray full of burgers. She rolled up to a station wagon, beaming at a family of four, oblivious to the fact that she had escaped death by mere inches.

When we got home, he stomped into the house without a word.

We followed him inside. I laid a hand on my brother's shoulder. I could hear his stomach growling.

"Sorry about that," I said.

"Don't touch me," Matthew said.

"What did I do?"

"You always wreck everything, then blame Dad."

"Matthew...you seriously think what happened at Ford's was *my* fault?"

"See what I mean? You don't even know."

Dad slammed a box of Corn Flakes down on the table in front of us. "Here you go, Mr. Fancypants. No tomatoes."

Matthew shot me a dirty look as our father stormed out of the room.

I watched him go. Matthew got a bowl and a spoon from the drainer beside the sink, and the milk from the fridge. He poured a mountain of cereal into the bowl. Took the lid off the milk and sniffed inside the jug. Made a face that suggested it was starting to go bad. Dumped what was left into his bowl anyway.

"I was only sticking up for you," I whispered.

"Whatever," he said. "Good thing you won't have to worry about that anymore."

"What's that supposed to mean?"

"I decided I'm not going."

"What?"

"You heard me."

"But we've been planning this since summer."

"*You've* been planning it."

I fought back tears. "But...you said you wanted to."

"I changed my mind."

"You think because Dad was gonna take you to your favorite restaurant, all of a sudden he's Father of the Year?"

"You act like living with Mom would be so much better. But what if he's right? What if she doesn't want us around?"

"He's wrong, Matthew. You were just a toddler when she left, so you don't remember her like I do, but...she loved us more than anything."

He brought a spoonful of Corn Flakes to his mouth and started chomping loudly. Milk dripped down his chin. "Dad said she left because she didn't want to be our momma anymore."

"Yeah, and he's *lying*."

"How do you know?"

"Because he's a liar."

"So are you. You lie *and* you steal."

"That's not fair. Everything I've done, it was for *you*. For us. You know that."

He shrugged.

"You wanna go to the park?"

"No," Matthew mumbled. "I'm hungry, and I got homework to do."

Dad entered the room then, and I quickly crossed the kitchen to get my own bowl and spoon. He had already changed out of his work coveralls into a dirty white T-shirt, blue boxers, and socks pulled up to his knees.

"What are you two jawing about?"

"Nothing," I said.

"Didn't sound like nothing. Sounded like secrets. You know we don't have secrets in this house."

"Stupid stuff," I said. "We were…arguing about whether Batman prefers Cocoa Pebbles or Cocoa Puffs."

"You're right," Dad said. "That *is* stupid. Shut up and eat your dinner."

He helped himself to a can of beer from the fridge and left the room again. Sometimes I thought the only thing that made him happier than hitting us was not having to see us at all.

"How could you even think about staying here with *that?*" I asked my brother, when Dad was out of earshot.

"I don't know," he said, "but I ain't going."

I started to say something else but decided against it. I didn't know what else to say anyway.

I filled my bowl with Corn Flakes. Tried to add milk, but Matthew had already emptied the jug.

I couldn't have drifted off for more than twenty or thirty minutes when the music woke us. I had been dreaming of my mother and a magical place called California. The albino buck was there too, I was sure, although I could not recall specific details of my dream.

My heart raced as I sat up in bed. Gordon Lightfoot's "Sundown" rattled the windows and vibrated through the walls of our home.

Dad preferred using cheap beer to pickle his liver. Two or three times a year, though, he would stop at the liquor store on his way home from work and buy a bottle of George Dickel Superior No. 12. It was almost as if he knew ahead of time that he would start thinking about Mom after dinner and would need something extra-potent to help him spiral downward. Throughout the night and into the wee hours of the morning, he would drain the bottle–straight, no chaser–and the soundtrack to his pain was always the same song. He had a small collection of old country records in the storage shed out back, but I'm pretty sure *Gord's Gold* was the only CD he owned. It never left the stereo in the corner of our living room, the one a family friend had traded to my father to pay off a bill for some auto repairs (most of its knobs were missing and there was a short in the electrical cord, but Dad boasted that he had gotten the sweet end of the deal). On the nights he drank liquor, he would play track twelve on repeat, over and over, as if "Sundown" was the only song Mr. Lightfoot had ever recorded. Dad wept and moaned so loudly we could hear him in there even though the music was turned up as loud as it would go, and it would continue into the wee hours of the morning.

"Oh, no." Matthew covered his ears. "Not again."

"Go back to sleep," I said. "Maybe he won't come in here."

"Jake, I'm scared."

"He'll probably just pass out. That's what he did last time."

"Yeah, but not the time before that…or the time before that."

I couldn't argue with him. The scorched sofa that stank up our storage shed was a casualty of Dad's last date with George Dickel. But that was nothing compared to one night the previous winter. He had called Matthew into the living room to harass him for leaving a bunch of his Matchbox cars on the floor. Matthew didn't respond promptly enough for his liking, because he was asleep. The little guy had worn a splint on his pinkie for the next two weeks. Dad didn't break Matthew's finger, only sprained it, but I feared we wouldn't dodge the proverbial bullet forever. We somehow convinced the doctor the injury had been the result of a bicycle accident, even though we had arrived at the E.R. around one o' clock in the morning and our father had smelled like a distillery. I often wondered afterward, as I lay awake at night pondering all the reasons we should run away, what story my brother or I would concoct to cover for him when Dad eventually killed one of us.

"You remember?" Matthew asked me.

"I remember. Just…keep quiet, okay? That's the best thing we can do."

"Okay."

We lay there for a long time. It might have been twenty minutes, or it might have been an hour. Meanwhile, Gordon Lightfoot sang on.

"Jake?" Matthew said.

"Yeah, buddy?"

"You think he passed out already?"

"Your guess is as good as mine."

"Can you go check? Please?"

"Shh."

The music played on, so loud I was surprised the police didn't come knocking at our front door. Surely Dad was in violation of some sort of local noise ordinance. But our closest neighbor lived a mile down the road, and he worked for a trucking company, so he was never home.

I threw back my blankets and swung my legs over the side of the bed.

"Wait here," I told Matthew. "Don't make a sound."

He blinked at me, shook his head. His face was painted an eerie orange by the glow of our Wolf Man nightlight.

I tiptoed out of the room and crept down the hall. Peeked into the living room…

…and breathed a sigh of relief. He was sprawled out in his favorite recliner, his head tilted back. His eyes were closed. His T-shirt had ridden up to expose his hairy belly. The picture of him and Mom on their wedding day–the one that normally sat atop the television–lay in his lap. His left hand was splayed on the cracked glass like a giant spider pinning my photo-mother down. The other was tucked into the front of his boxers. His whiskey glass lay on its side next to his chair; a small puddle of the amber-colored liquid had soaked into the carpet.

I pushed the power button on the stereo. The house went silent, except for a metallic ticking from the radiator beneath the windowsill. I stood as still as a statue for a minute or more, waiting for a reaction from my father. Gordon Lightfoot leered at me from the dusty CD cover that lay atop one speaker, and I loathed him.

I approached Dad's chair. He was a big man, six feet tall and well over two hundred pounds, but as I gazed down at him now he looked pathetic. His head twitched. His right hand slid out of his boxers, hovered in the air for a moment as if he was beckoning to someone in his sleep. He smacked his lips, mumbled something that sounded like a line from the Gordon Lightfoot song he loved so much.

I wondered what it would feel like to place a pillow over his face, to hold it there while he struggled…until he didn't struggle anymore.

Slowly, I slid the photo out from under his hand. He had been kissing her again, I could tell. Mom's face was hidden by a smear of his saliva. The effect was like a video in which a person's features are blurred to conceal her identity.

I wiped the mess off the photo, onto the arm of his chair.

He smacked his lips again. Farted. It smelled like Vienna sausages.

I returned the photo to its place atop the TV and went back to my room, where Matthew sat sucking his thumb and awaiting my report.

"He's sawing logs," I said as I climbed under the covers, "like we ought to be. It's late."

"Jake?"

"What is it, squirt?"

"I changed my mind. I'll go with you. I don't want to be anywhere without you."

"Good to hear." I grinned in the darkness. "I don't want to be anywhere without *you*."

CHAPTER SEVEN

Two days later. A Thursday morning. I was busy making baloney sandwiches for our lunches while Matthew finished a glass of orange juice and a piece of toast smeared with apple butter. I had burned the toast, but he didn't seem to mind.

"It's almost eight o' clock," my brother said around a mouthful of his breakfast. "We're gonna be late. Should we make sure Dad's awake?"

"Be my guest," I said.

"Nah. I'm good."

As if on cue, Dad walked in then, shrugging into his wrinkled work shirt ("KURT'S AUTOMOTIVE" read the logo embroidered over his heart). His unwashed hair stuck up on either side of his head like devil's horns. He smelled as if he had bathed in the cheap cologne he always wore.

I noticed his pants were unzipped, but I didn't say anything. The thought of him walking around all day talking to his customers with his fly hanging open filled me with a sick thrill.

"Forgot to set my alarm," he said. "Here's a note for your teachers."

He reached into his breast pocket and pulled out two pieces of paper. He handed one to each of us. He had scribbled "EXCUSE MY SON FOR BEING LATE AND HE WANT BE THEIR MONDAY" in pencil on the backs of two old receipts for auto parts.

"Shop number's on there if they got any questions."

"Okay," I said.

"Okay," Matthew said.

"I gotta put in a new transmission first thing, promised Steve Thompson it'd be done two days ago. Think you boys can catch the Public Transit bus like you did last time?"

"Sure," I said.

Dad's lips parted as if he were about to say something else, but whatever it was he decided it against it. He picked up Matthew's glass and downed the last dregs of pulpy OJ left at the bottom. He handed the empty glass back to Matthew. Nodded at us before turning to leave the room.

I heard the front door slam a few seconds later.

"Hurry up and finish your breakfast." I threw our sandwiches into paper bags with chips and juice boxes. "This is it."

I ran to the living room window, watched Dad climb into his truck. He started the engine. It backfired, then rolled out of the driveway and headed down the road, crapping blue smoke in its wake. I ran back to the kitchen, where Matthew was dropping his dirty dishes into the sink.

"What are you doing?" he asked me.

"We leave to go hunting tomorrow. I have to get those comic books, and I have to sell them *today*."

"What about school?"

"We've got the note from Dad. A few more minutes won't hurt. When we get there, you'll go to class like normal. I can be back in time for the lunch bell."

"You're gonna *cut class?*"

"It'll be okay," I said. "Go stand watch, in case he comes back!"

"Sir, yes, sir!" He gave me a stiff-armed salute and sprinted down the hallway.

I fell to my hands and knees by Dad's bed. First things first, I plugged the cord to his alarm clock back into the wall. It had been a risky move, sneaking into his bedroom to unplug it after I heard his chainsaw snore rev up through the thin wall between our rooms (I was sure my heart skipped several beats when I had knocked over the empty beer bottle sitting on his nightstand). Now I couldn't believe how easy it had been.

When that was done, I reached under his bed and pulled out a small metal footlocker. It was olive green with a faded NRA sticker stuck to its lid. I flipped up the clasps, opened it.

Inside lay Grandpa's comics. Dozens of them, with titles ranging from *Justice League of America* to *The Astonishing X-Men*, from *Batman* to *The Incredible Hulk*, from *The Green Lantern* to *The Amazing Spider-Man*, from *The Flash* to *The Fantastic Four*. *Sgt. Rock* had obviously been his favorite–presumably because Grandpa had been a military man himself–as this title was most prevalent throughout the stack. He had taken immaculate care of his collection through the years. Every one of his books was stored in a clear plastic bag with a stiff white backing board, just like the ones behind the counter at Heroes n' More on Tenth Street.

I tried but realized right away that I couldn't fit all of them in my backpack. That wouldn't be a problem, however. I had done my research the day before. I had found a copy of the *Overstreet Comic Book Price Guide* in my school library. It was almost twenty years out-of-date, but that meant the books were worth even more now. Thanks to Grandpa, Matthew and I would soon have enough money to get away from our father for good. The crimefighters in his collection could shoot lasers out of their eyes, they hefted eighteen-wheelers above their heads with no more effort than lifting a feather, and they soared through the air at the speed of sound. Our grandfather had never worn spandex, as far as I knew, and he had been in the grave for a decade. But he was *our* superhero.

Although I had admired Grandpa's comics many times before and had read each of them from cover to cover at least once, I took a moment to admire my booty like a pirate who has finally found that elusive chest full of buried treasure.

I slid a third of the stack into my backpack, closed the locker, and shoved it back under the bed.

Matthew and I were walking through the park on our way to the bus stop at the top of the hill, sharing with each other all the things we couldn't wait to say to Mom once we were reunited, when everything went bad.

My heart skipped a beat. My guts roiled. How could I have been so *stupid?* I should have been on high alert. Should have known that cutting class was something new to me, but for a guy like Caleb Caldwell it was the norm. I had really screwed this up. With everything else going on–my rush to sell the comics, the hunting trip coming up in less than thirty-six hours, the fear that Dad might somehow discover our plan before we got away–I had failed to see my archenemy sitting on the swing-set in the middle of the park.

Today, there were only two of them, but that didn't make me feel any better. Caleb had on a wrinkled Metallica t-shirt and blue jeans with mud stains on the knees. His NC State baseball cap was turned backwards. Austin wore a Lakers jersey and, despite the autumn chill in the air, silver shorts that came down to his shins. Caleb coughed into his fist while Austin sucked on the end of a small metal pipe.

I could smell the sweet stench of their marijuana from a hundred feet away.

"Hey, faggots!" Caleb shouted, as they started walking toward us.

"Oh, no," said Matthew. "What are we gonna do?"

"I'll tell you what we're gonna do..."

I took another three or four tentative steps before I knew the answer.

"...we're gonna *run!*"

I grabbed my brother's hand, and we made for Crites Road. Although I didn't like our chances either way, the bus stop was closer than the woods.

We didn't dare look back. I could hear their breaths behind us, their footfalls like those of giants rampaging across the Earth. My backpack jostled against my kidneys, heavy with textbooks and Grandpa's precious comics.

They caught up with us at the bottom of the hill.

One of them shoved me from behind. I went down hard, ate a face-full of dirt.

Matthew screamed my name, ran to my side as I rolled over.

I sat up. Spat dirt and grass from my mouth as I crab-walked backward, away from the advancing bullies.

"Skipping school, shitheads?" Caleb said as he strutted closer. I noticed he had lost his baseball cap during the pursuit, but if he knew it he didn't care.

Austin cracked his knuckles in anticipation of what came next.

Caleb reached to his side, unsnapped a leather sheath, and pulled out a large Bowie knife. He started waving it back and forth between us.

"How you like *that?*" he asked me.

It was a nice knife. I owned a smaller version myself. But mine was at home, in a shoebox under my bed. A lot of good it did me now.

"Really, asshole?" I said. "You gonna stab me? You wanna go to jail?"

"Maybe I don't care," he said. "Maybe it'd be worth it to kill a little pussy like you."

Austin laughed.

"What do you think, Austin? Where should I cut this faggot first?"

"You should cut his pecker off and make him eat it."

"I would, but he ain't got a pecker."

"Leave him alone!" Matthew cried.

"Shut up, you little queer," said Caleb, stabbing the knife into the air in Matthew's direction.

Matthew shrank back.

Brakes squealed at the top of the hill. I glanced back, saw the Public Transit bus rolling to a stop near the entrance to the park. On the side of the vehicle was a large ad for GRANDDAD'S DAIRY, LLC.

"Matthew," I said. "Get on the bus!"

He stared at me, trembling.

"Go! Get out of here!"

My brother ran for the bus stop, his sobs echoing behind him as he fled.

"Don't just stand there," Caleb said to Austin. "Get him!"

Austin chased after Matthew. He was at least thirty pounds overweight, though, kept stopping to pull up his shorts as he ran, and my brother had a good head-start.

I leapt to my feet and swung my backpack at Caleb as hard as I could.

He saw it coming, blocked it with the hand that was holding the knife.

The blade stabbed through the middle of my backpack.

"No!" I screamed.

He tugged at his knife, trying to pull it out. It was stuck tight, like some white-trash Excalibur.

For the next few seconds, we engaged in a violent tug-of-war...

...and somehow, I won. I gave one final, violent yank, tumbled backward. My ass hit the ground. My backpack thumped on the ground beside me, and Caleb's knife fell out.

Caleb roared as he tackled me. My breath burst out of me in a *woof*! I fought to get away, but he straddled my waist, pinning me to the ground. He balled one hand into a fist and smiled down at me, savoring my fear.

"No," I cried. "Please..."

He thought I was begging for mercy. He was wrong. My head rolled to one side, and even as he prepared to pound my face into raw hamburger, I could only stare at my backpack—with that awful, ragged hole in the middle—lying in the dirt beside me.

"You fucking pussy," he said. "Now I'm gonna give you something to *really* cry about..."

I slammed my hand into his crotch and squeezed.

Caleb shrieked, rolled off me. Gasped for air as he held himself through his jeans.

I scrambled to my feet. Grabbed the backpack by one strap.

Caleb rose too, albeit on wobbly legs.

"You...are so...dead," he wheezed.

I desperately glanced around for something to use as a weapon. The knife was nowhere in sight.

I spotted a broken branch on the ground. It was the size and shape of a baseball bat; one end was covered in furry green moss. I stumbled forward, picked it up...

...and broke it in two upside Caleb's head as he lunged for me again.

He babbled something nonsensical before crumpling to the ground.

I ran for the bus stop. Passed Austin on the way. He staggered down the hill, calling Caleb's name. He sounded like he might start crying. I ignored him. He ignored me.

I watched the bus pull away from the curb. Matthew stared at me from behind a window, his hand pressed to the glass. He mouthed my name, and I gave him a shaky thumbs-up: *I'm okay, squirt. Everything's okay...*

Everything wasn't okay, though.

I stared down at the hole in my backpack. It was small, didn't go all the way through. But it didn't matter.

My father was the kind of man who believed that crying was for little girls. It was a sign of weakness, he had told me on more than one occasion. I would be lying if I said I didn't think about that any time I felt the need to show my emotions. I still struggle with it today.

Nevertheless, I began to sob as I ran toward town. I feared I might never stop crying, and I couldn't care less who saw me along the way.

CHAPTER EIGHT

"I'm sorry, pal," said the owner of Heroes n' More. "There's just not much I can do with books in this condition."

My shoulders slumped. I stared down at my stack of ruined comics on the counter between us and their covers grew blurry as my already red and swollen eyes filled with new tears.

"This can't be happening," I said, my voice cracking.

"You gotta understand where I'm coming from, Jake. I mean, most of these look like you had a run-in with my man, Wolverine! You had some sweet books here, and I would have loved to take 'em off your hands, but…I'm really sorry, bud."

Ronnie "Round Man" Miller was an obese fellow with a Marine-style buzz-cut and a bushy salt-and-pepper goatee that dangled to his chest. He favored loud Hawaiian shirts and leather sandals, wore three silver hoops in his left ear. I liked Round Man a lot, and although I never felt comfortable calling him that to his face, he scolded me when I didn't, and would threaten to start charging me for coming into his shop and reading his comics without buying anything (something he never complained about otherwise). He was a genuinely nice guy, always striking up conversations with his customers about the latest Doom Patrol story arc or which of his favorite books was next to be butchered by Hollywood. His store was my favorite place in the world. Matthew and I would drop by at least once a month to thumb through the new releases and to stare at the expensive maquettes in their glass case along the back wall (my personal favorites: Spider-Man slinging a sticky web from his wrist, Daredevil brooding atop a gargoyle's rocky snout, and a curvaceous Catwoman wielding her whip while an army of felines brushed against her ankles). We envied the kids who could afford to purchase Round Man's wares, and we always looked forward to that one day of the year when we felt as if we belonged to their elite club: the first Saturday in May. Free Comic Book Day was our Christmas.

I was saddened when I heard a few years ago that Round Man's shop had burned to the ground due to a faulty space heater. It was as if a large part of my childhood went up in smoke, literally. Last I heard, he had moved upstate, where he now owns a convenience store.

"There's nothing you can do for me?" I asked him. "I'll take anything, Round Man. I really need some money..."

I could feel my plans slipping through my fingers like fine sand turned to mud.

"Jake," said Round Man, "is everything okay? I mean, if you're in some kinda trouble, maybe I could help?"

"Please just buy my books," I said.

He made a clucking sound with his tongue, shook his head. Rested one hairy elbow on the countertop between us. He fanned out the stack of comics I had taken from my grandfather's footlocker, and as he gave them a closer inspection they snagged on one another due to the puckered hole through the middle of at least two thirds of them. Round Man winced, as if seeing such precious stock reduced to four-color garbage caused him physical pain.

He wasn't the only one. I turned away, ran my fingers through my sweat-damp hair, and swallowed back the urge to vomit on the seven-foot *Alien* xenomorph statue in the middle of the room ("PLEASE DON'T TOUCH" read the placard at its base). A life-sized bust of Batman glared at me from a shelf a few feet away. *Consider this a lesson learned,* the Caped Crusader admonished me from beneath his cowl, *crime does* not *pay.*

I thumbed tears from my eyes. Everywhere I looked there was a shiny comic book in mint condition. In one corner stood a display advertising products that would "PROTECT YOUR COMICS!!!" None of the collector's jargon made sense to me (mylar bags...polyethylene bags...acid-free boards "buffered with 3% calcium carbonate"), but it didn't matter anyway because nothing could make a bully's knife bounce off your books like bullets bounced off Superman's chest.

"Here's the deal," Round Man said. "I can't do anything with *Batman* #251, that's for sure. Same for your *Uncanny X-Men* #129–it's not the rarest book in existence, but it's still a darn shame 'cause that was the first appearance of both Kitty Pryde and the Hellfire Club." He hissed through his teeth. "Looks like all your *Justice League*s are toast as well."

"Yeah," I said. "I know."

But then he segregated a few books from the rest of the stack, those that had been on the bottom of the pile when I slid them inside my backpack. Perhaps a dozen of them had avoided being skewered by Caleb's knife, when it didn't go all the way through.

Round Man stroked his massive goatee, as if it helped him concentrate, before crossing his arms in front of his chest. "Tell you what. I can offer you two hundred and fifty smackaroonies for the rest of these. Best I can do."

"It's a deal!" I almost shouted.

He stuck out a meaty hand. We shook on it.

He waddled over to his cash register. There was a Captain America sticker on one side of the machine; Round Man had taped a photo of his own face over Cap's head. There was another one on the opposite side–Round Man as Obi-Wan Kenobi, replete with robe and lightsaber. He punched a few buttons and the register's drawer popped open.

"Never seen anybody so anxious to unload a few comics," he said. "You planning to ditch town or something?"

He chuckled. I didn't.

"Well, don't spend it all in one place. And take better care of your comics. They're an investment, my friend."

As he counted off the bills into my palm, I began to cry again. Tears of joy, this time.

Two hundred and fifty bucks. It was exactly five dollars more than I needed for our tickets to California.

CHAPTER NINE

I attacked my dinner like a lion devouring a gazelle. It had been a long day full of emotional highs and lows, and I was nothing less than ravenous. Not to mention the fact that the food smelled delicious. Dad had cooked for us, a rare occurrence to say the least: a pot of chili and grilled-cheese sandwiches.

"Jake?" he said. "You forgetting something, son?"

My face grew hot. "Sorry."

We bowed our heads and Dad mumbled a quick prayer: "For what we are about to enjoy, may the Lord make us truly grateful."

"Amen," Matthew said.

"Amen," I said.

We dug in.

A minute later, there was a knock at the door.

"Who could that be?" Dad grunted. A string of cheese hung from his bottom lip.

My brother and I exchanged a worried look.

"Jake, get the door. Whoever it is, tell 'em to piss off. This is family time."

I hurried to the front door. Opened it without asking who it was. I did that a lot back then, and Dad used to fuss at me for it. But the way I saw it, the possibility was slim that the person on the other side might be someone I feared more than my own father…

My breath caught in my throat when I saw the sheriff standing on our porch.

She stood beneath the yellowish glow of our porch light, her hands behind her back. She wore a khaki uniform and a massive gun on her hip that instantly captured my attention. Her reddish-brown hair was tied back in a ponytail. The tiny emerald studs in her ears matched her bright green eyes. She wasn't much taller than me. She was in her mid-forties, but, when she offered me a warm smile, she looked ten years younger. Dad despised Theresa McLelland. Perhaps it was because he had been lifelong friends with her predecessor. However, based on some of the things I had heard him say after she won the election two years ago, I suspected it was due to more than a hint of misogyny (when one of her deputies pulled up in our driveway the night he burned our sofa he asked if "Dickless Tracy" was at home changing her tampon). I always thought she seemed so kind, any time I saw her around town, and I could never understand Dad's disdain for Sheriff McLelland.

"Hey there. You're Jacob, right?"

"Um...yeah, that's right."

"Is your dad home, Jacob?"

"Yes, ma'am."

"Could you run and get him for me?"

"Yes, ma'am."

When I told Dad it was "the cops," he took a sip of beer, then wiped his mouth with a paper towel. Scooted his chair back from the table and mumbled something about how it didn't take much to make his good mood fly right out the friggin' window. He took his sweet time making his way to the door.

I lingered in the hallway outside the kitchen, eavesdropping on their conversation.

"Mr. Bradersen?" said the sheriff.

"Kurt Bradersen, that's me. What do you need...officer?" He said the word as if it were an insult.

McLelland's middle finger tapped the badge pinned to her chest. "It's *Sheriff*, actually. Mr. Bradersen, I'm here to talk to you about a young man named Caleb Caldwell. He was seriously injured this morning, and it appears–"

"What's that gotta do with me?" Dad interrupted her.

"Well, sir, the evidence suggests Caleb was attacked. It appears he was struck in the head with a heavy object. Like a stick."

"He say I did it?"

"No, sir. But I did want to ask y–"

"I'll make sure to say a prayer for the kid this Sunday. Right now, I'm trying to eat my supper."

"I'll let you get back to that as soon as possible," said the sheriff. "But first...I've heard there's some history between Caleb Caldwell and your oldest son?"

"Boy's daddy tell you that?"

"He did."

"They used to have a problem. I talked to Bob Caldwell about it. Now they don't."

"I see. Mr. Bradersen, would you mind telling me where you were this morning around nine a.m.?"

"I was at work. Got a line of customers who can back me up. Talk to Steve Thompson. Brett Tucker. You need more names? I got 'em."

"Can you attest to Jacob's whereabouts?"

Dad stared at her, didn't have an answer for that one. The question hung between them for a long, awkward moment. The furnace kicked on with a low hum. Matthew asked me through a mouthful of chili what was going on, and I gestured for him to be quiet. Dad glanced back over his shoulder at me, and I ducked out of sight.

Finally, he said, "Jacob was in school. Where he shoulda been."

"You sure about that?" asked Sheriff McLelland.

Dad cleared his throat. Shifted his weight from one foot to the other. "Of course, I'm sure. You insinuating I don't know what my own son gets up to?"

"Of course not, sir. A young man was assaulted today, and I'm just doing my job. Trying to gather all the facts."

Dad gave a noncommittal grunt.

"May I come in?" the sheriff asked him. "I'd really like to speak with your–"

"No, you may not," Dad replied. "Now, if you don't mind, *sheriff*, my supper's getting cold."

He stepped back and closed the door in her face.

Dad plopped back down at the table. Started to shovel a spoonful of chili into his mouth. But he paused when the spoon was an inch from his lips.

"Something happen between you and the Caldwell boy?" he asked me.

I stared down at my plate.

"I asked you a question, Jake."

I nodded.

"You hurt him?"

I shrugged. But then nodded again.

He set down his spoon. "I always told you what would happen if you went around starting fights."

"Yes, sir."

"But I also told you…if somebody's picking on you, you damn sure better end it."

"I did," I said.

"Good," Dad said, before digging in again.

CHAPTER TEN

On Friday evening, we made a trip to the grocery store for supplies after Dad picked us up from school. From there we would head straight to the cabin. Our stuff was already packed for the trip and waiting in the back of the truck.

"Matthew," Dad said, as he pushed the cart down the potato chip aisle, "run and pick up a couple packs of wieners outta the meat section."

"Wieners," Matthew giggled.

"Yeah," said Dad.

My brother ran off. Dad and I threw a few more things into the cart: a bag of chips, a bag of cheese puffs, an eight-pack of hot dog buns. Overhead, on the store's P.A. system, Billy Joel sang "Only the Good Die Young."

After a few minutes, Dad said, "What the hell's taking your brother so long?"

We caught up with Matthew in the meat department. He was chatting with a teacher he knew from school. He said goodbye to her as we approached. I noticed my father turned to admire her backside as she walked away, but then he wrinkled up his nose as if he didn't like what he saw.

Matthew stuck two packages of brand-name wieners in his face, beaming like a kid who had just won first place in a spelling bee.

Dad snatched them out of his hands, threw them back into the cold case, and chose a generic brand instead. "You think I'm made of money?"

Matthew sniffled but said nothing. I wrapped one arm around him as we walked, patted him on the shoulder.

"Jake," Dad said, "go get some matches. The wooden kind. Make sure they're 'strike anywhere.' That's important. It'll say it on the box."

"Sure thing," I said.

I would get his matches. But first, I planned to take a detour. I had been waiting for a chance to do some shopping of my own.

I grabbed the first box I saw. It was blue and white, had a picture on the front of a chubby cartoon man dozing on a fluffy cloud, a contented grin on his face. The pills were called 3-2-1-ZZZ's.

I took a deep breath, let it out slowly. Stared down at the box and thought, *I can't believe we're really gonna do this.*

I shoved the sleeping pills down the front of my pants then, with the wad of money I had been saving all year. The bills were held together with a rubber band and tucked inside a piece of yellow paper folded in half. The paper was a page that I had ripped out of the phonebook before we left the house. "GO GREYHOUND AND LEAVE THE DRIVING TO US!" read the ad, above the address and phone number of the closest depot.

Next I went looking for some matches. I snatched a box of strike-anywheres from the shelf before running to find my family.

I found them in the checkout line. They stood behind a stooped old woman who was counting change from her purse to pay for a bottle of cooking sherry. Matthew looked bored out of his mind. So did the young lady behind the register. Dad looked annoyed.

"What took you so long?" Dad's forehead was shiny with sweat. I could tell he needed a drink.

"I, uh, had trouble finding the matches," I said.

"Figured. I already got 'em. You want something done right you might as well do it yourself. Put those back and let's go. I wanna get to the cabin before dark."

CHAPTER ELEVEN

Dad's shop was a cinderblock building on the edge of town. On the left was an office with a large bay window that reflected the lumberyard across the street; on the right were two garage doors. Over the roll-up doors, a sign made of wooden planks read "KURT'S AUTOMOTIVE," blood-red letters on a white background. The shop sat beside a storage lot packed with RVs, boats, and stacks of old tires. A gold 1965 Oldsmobile Cutlass with a "FOR SALE" sign in the window was parked at the front of the lot.

As Dad pulled up near the office, I pointed at the Cutlass.

"Why is my car for sale?" I asked him.

"What do you mean *your* car?"

"Grandpa's Cutlass. You said you were going to fix it up for me. You said I could have it when I turn sixteen."

Dad gave a mean chuckle. "I said that? I musta been drunk."

God, how I despised him.

"You don't want that thing anyway, Jake. It gets about two gallons to the mile. Cutlass is for show, not for driving."

I wondered if he would say that to the next person who inquired about the "FOR SALE" sign.

He killed the engine, told us to stay in the truck. He had to get the guns out of the safe, then take care of one last thing.

"It won't be long now," I said to Matthew, once Dad was out of earshot.

He came out with two black nylon rifle bags slung over his shoulder. He approached the passenger side of the truck, made a gesture for me to roll down the window.

He blushed as he handed me a black Magic Marker and a piece of notebook paper. "I, uh, need you to make my sign for me."

"What should it say?" I asked him.

"CLOSED TIL TUESDAY. No...GONE HUNTING. Under that write SEE YOU NEXT TUESDAY."

"Okay."

He watched while I followed his instructions. "You got your good looks from me, but that fancy handwriting you got from your mama."

He taped the sign to the door when I was finished, over a yellowed poster advertising Valvoline motor oil, and locked the place up.

"What now?" I said, when he was back behind the wheel.

"We go hunting," Dad replied.

CHAPTER TWELVE

The woods flew by on the other side of my cracked window. The asphalt hummed beneath the truck's tires. Dad's foot was heavy on the gas pedal, as always. I didn't realize I had been singing along beneath my breath with the Bob Seger song on the radio until I looked over to see Dad watching me with one cocked eyebrow. He chuckled and I stopped.

"Won't be long now," he said.

I felt a chill, remembering how I had said those same words to Matthew back at the shop.

We passed a sign: OLD JUNCTION 9 NEXT LEFT.

"How far is it?" I asked Dad.

"We'll be there in half an hour, maybe? We get to Steck's Mill, it's three or four miles 'til we cross the river. Camp's another ten miles past that."

"Cool," I said.

He slowed, but only a little, to take the turn onto Old Junction 9.

The sun began to dip below the horizon, painting the heavens in streaks of pink and purple.

STECK'S MILL, POP. 1689 read the bullet-riddled sign by the side of the road. It sat in front of a sprawling lumber factory, as if town and factory were one and the same. In the center of it all a massive black smokestack stabbed the evening sky like a colossal birdie finger.

The lights of Steck's Mill receded into the twilight. A few minutes later, the pickup rattled over a wooden bridge. A pair of dark figures–a man and his floppy-eared dog–shuffled along the side. In the gathering darkness, the river resembled an obsidian mirror a hundred feet below us.

"Steck's Mill," I said. "Isn't that where Grandpa was from?"

"Back in the sixties, most of the land around here belonged to our family," Dad said. "A lot has changed since then."

He didn't explain further, and I didn't ask him to.

Before long, we reached an area where the trees grew taller and thicker. The shadows were longer and darker. I thought of the fairytales Mom used to tell me before bed, of black forests haunted by old hags hungry for the bones of small children. I felt a chill, but I wasn't sure if it was because of Mom's stories or the knowledge of what Matthew and I planned to do once we reached our destination.

Dad turned right onto a rutted trail, and the truck's headlights revealed a heavy chain blocking our path. It was attached to a concrete cylinder on each side of the road. A sign dangled from the middle of the chain: "PRIVATE PROPERTY/NO TRESPASSING."

He stopped but left the engine running. He opened the ashtray beneath the dashboard, pulled out a small brass key I had never known was in there. He climbed out of the truck, unlocked a padlock and the chain fell away. He climbed in again, pulled forward about fifteen feet, then got out to put the chain back in place.

We drove on down the trail. Behind us, the truck's taillights lit up the night as if the world had turned blood-red in our wake.

Dad steered around a deep curve, and the high beams swept across another dirt road branching off to the right. We veered to the left.

A few minutes later we came to another fork in the road. This time we went right.

Then another left.

I watched, trying to memorize every turn. Matthew and I would have to find our way out of here, eventually. And by then it would be full dark.

"Dad?" I said.

"Yeah?"

"Where do the other roads lead?"

"To different parts of the property."

"Other cabins?" Matthew asked.

"Nope. Your grandfather planned to build more originally, thought he might rent 'em out, but he only finished the one before your grandma got sick and he had to start selling off his land to pay for her doctor bills."

"That sucks," I said.

Dad shifted in his seat, winced as if he were in pain. I could tell the conversation had conjured up some bad memories for him. His grip tightened on the steering wheel. "Quit asking so many questions, you two. You're giving me a headache."

"Yes, sir," Matthew and I said at the same time.

I watched him shift gears again as we headed down a steep hill. Gravel crunched beneath the pickup's tires now.

At last, we arrived at the cabin. It sat in a wide, circular clearing. Its walls were painted a dark forest green. It wasn't much smaller than our house back home. Four concrete steps led up to a slender front porch beneath a steep metal roof. The porch was furnished with three steel chairs and a small card table. Atop the railing sat three old flower pots; whatever had been planted inside of them was now dead and brown. The cabin's windows resembled two eyes gazing back at us as the truck's headlights were reflected in their glass. A wooden sign with our surname burned into it was mounted over the front door.

Dad parked the truck and we all got out. But not before I took a deep, calming breath.

"Everything okay, Jake?" asked Dad.

"Everything's great," I said.

"You seem kinda antsy."

"Just excited," I said. "Can't wait to go hunting."

"That a boy." He stretched his arms and legs. I heard his joints pop. "I wanna check on the generator first, make sure it has plenty of gas. We'll get a nice fire going before we unload the gear."

"Cool," I said.

But what I thought was: *And then you're gonna take a little nap…*

Dad squatted down in front of the old-timey woodstove, struck a match and held the flame to a pile of crumpled newspaper under a stack of kindling. He blew on it until he got the fire going. He held his hands out to bask in the heat for a minute, made a satisfied noise in the back of his throat.

When he turned around, he caught me staring at a photo on the wall. It was displayed in a dusty wooden frame between an antique frying pan and the same .257 Winchester Model 70 that I had turned on my father in my dream a few nights ago. The albino buck stood slightly left-of-center in the photo, its rear haunches hidden by a bush polka-dotted with berries the same color as the animal's ghostly eyes. The photo had been taken hastily, but the image was clear enough; this was no grainy Patterson-Gimlin production, the blurred video that purported to prove the existence of Bigfoot. The albino buck was real, he was out there, and whoever snapped the picture had spotted the majestic beast from less than thirty yards away.

"Is that how he looked in your dream?" Dad asked me.

"Pretty much," I said.

"He's a beaut, ain't he?"

"How many times have you seen him?"

"Half a dozen, maybe?"

I suspected some exaggeration on his part. Knowing my father, he would have been carrying a hunting rifle every time he came up here, and if he had seen the buck while he was armed, he would have killed it without hesitation. Its enormous rack would have been mounted on our living room wall back home, above the television. Perhaps he would have hung his keys from its tines, or his JESUS IS MY CO-PILOT cap with the fishhook on the bill.

He walked over to stand beside me, tapped the picture with a knuckle. "That was the last time. Haven't seen him since."

"You think he's still alive?"

"Oh, yeah," Dad said. "He's still alive." He offered no further explanation for how he was so sure.

I noticed he had tears in his eyes.

"Dad? You okay?"

"Just remembered your mama took that picture. A few days before she ran off."

I didn't say anything.

He quickly turned away. "I gotta take a piss. You and your brother start unloading the truck."

"Yes, sir."

I continued to stare at the photo for another minute or more before moving on to admire Grandpa's rifle on its mount upon the wall. Like his comics, I had been told that the Winchester would one day be mine. Dad had also mentioned, though, that he wasn't sure if the gun would even fire anymore ("Damn thing would probably blow up in your face if you tried," he said, "like everything else that's pretty on the outside"). It was covered from stock to barrel with a thin sheen of dust. I blew on it. Sneezed.

A strange sound startled me from my reverie then. It was a high-pitched bleating noise, reminded me of a cross between a duck's quack and the frogs that croaked behind our house in the summer.

It took me a moment before I realized it was Matthew playing with the deer call. I ran to the window, saw him standing on the back of the truck, blowing on it like Miles Davis performing a trumpet solo.

I hurried out there to tell him to stop before Dad caught him messing around with the gear.

We sat on the front porch, eating hot dogs and chips off paper plates. I wasn't hungry, but I knew I had to act normal, so I cleaned my plate along with Dad and Matthew. The food lay in my stomach like a lead weight. I asked Matthew more than once to quit talking with his mouth full, he told me to mind my own business, and Dad said we'd both better knock it off or we were cruisin' for a bruisin'.

When we were finished, Dad wiped his hands on his shirt, let out a long belch that echoed through the clearing like the mating call of some primal beast.

Matthew giggled. I faked a laugh of my own.

Dad tipped back his bottle of beer, emptied it in several swallows.

And then he said what I had been waiting to hear...

"Which one of you dudes wants to fetch your old man another brewski?"

I jumped up and said a bit too eagerly, "I'll do it!"

I felt Matthew watching me as I darted into the cabin. The screen door slammed behind me.

With trembling hands, I unzipped my backpack. Took out the box of sleeping pills. I tore open the box, dropped the package twice before I got it open. I pinched out two of the pills. Hesitated. *How many? He's been drinking. I don't want to kill him, just put him out of commission for a while...*

I peeled back the foil and tapped two more into my palm.

I ran to the kitchen area, used the handle of my miniature Bowie knife to crush the pills into powder on the counter, then popped the cap off a beer with a bottle opener.

"What's the holdup, Jake?" I heard Dad yell outside.

"Where's the bottle opener?" I shouted back.

"It's a twist-off, son. Use that big brain of yours."

"Got it."

"That's another thing you inherited from your mama," he chuckled. "A lack of common sense."

"Screw you," I said beneath my breath, as I dumped the pill dust down into the bottle.

CHAPTER THIRTEEN

Dad's snore filled the room. The fire crackled in the stove a few feet away.

Hauling him inside had been a lot harder than I had anticipated. My hair was stiff with sweat. Matthew's was too. My arms shook as we finished binding him to an old elbow chair with three coils of pumpkin-colored drag rope. Normally the rope was used for pulling a deer out of the woods after a hunter made his kill–Dad once told me those things could weigh up to three hundred pounds, and depending on where you set up your stand, you might have to haul their dead weight through the woods for a mile or more–so I had no doubt it would work just fine for the task at hand.

"I can't believe we're doing this, I can't believe we're doing this," Matthew babbled over and over.

"Make sure it's as tight as we can get it around his wrists and ankles," I said.

When we were finished, we stood back and admired our handiwork.

"What are we gonna do to him now?" Matthew asked me. "We're not gonna hurt him, are we?"

"What? Of course not. This is just to keep him restrained while we make a run for it."

"Okay."

I hoped the disappointment in my brother's eyes was a figment of my imagination. Hoped what we were doing here wouldn't warp him for the rest of his life. Was it too late? Had our father screwed us up beyond repair already? I could only pray we wouldn't one day end up just like Dad. But the praying would have to come later.

"I almost forgot something," I said.

I ran into the kitchen area and rummaged through some drawers until I found a roll of duct tape. I cut off a piece.

There was no one for miles around. No one to hear him when the pills wore off and he began to yell for help. Maybe I did it just to be mean.

I slapped the tape across his mouth.

He grunted. His right hand clenched into a fist, gripped the bottom of my shirt.

I yelped. Matthew and I jumped back. I heard my shirttail rip.

Dad's head rolled back, and he started snoring again.

"Whoa," Matthew said.

"Yeah," I said.

My little brother stared at me, awaiting my next move.

"Well," I said. "I guess that's that."

I grabbed Dad's keys off the hook by the door, and we got out of there.

CHAPTER FOURTEEN

I stabbed the key into the ignition. Turned it.

The truck started with a growl. It was the sweetest sound I had ever heard. It was the sound of *freedom*.

The engine sputtered and died.

No…

"You're sure you know how to drive?" Matthew's pale face judged me in the darkness.

"He showed me at the shop one time," I said. "With Grandpa's car. *My* car."

He obviously didn't believe me.

I cranked it again. The truck roared to life. I slammed it into gear. It lurched forward…and died.

"Crap!"

"Lemme guess…you *meant* to do that?"

"Shut up. This is harder than I thought. Grandpa's car only has two pedals."

"Jake–"

"It's okay. I'll figure it out."

"Well, you better hurry."

"Just be quiet for a minute!"

"This was a bad idea, Jake."

"Yeah, well, it's too late to turn back now."

I closed my eyes. Pressed down on the clutch and turned the key.

The engine backfired. Caught. The steering wheel vibrated in my grip like something with a mind of its own.

Yes!

I eased off the pedals. The truck lurched forward…and died again.

"Okay," I said.

"Okay what?" said Matthew.

"I *don't* know how to drive this thing."

Matthew started crying.

"Don't cry. We'll just start walking. Get the flashlight from behind the seat. Dad's not going anywhere, and nobody will have a clue we're missing until Tuesday morning at the soonest. By then we'll be in California with Mom."

He gazed up at me with tears glistening on his cheeks.

"Palm trees. Movie stars. And *no Dad*. Sounds pretty awesome, right?"

He wiped his eyes on his sleeve, smiled around his thumb, and said, "Right."

"First things first. Hold the light for me, squirt…"

I gave him the flashlight. It was one of those big heavy-duty spotlights with a handle on top. I slid my knife out of my hip pocket. Stabbed the blade into the front tire. The air hissed out and the truck sagged forward like a knight taking a knee before his king. I jogged around to the other side, did it again. Then again.

Matthew said, "Can I do one?"

"No," I said. "You'll hurt yourself."

"Aww." He kicked at the gravel halfheartedly.

After the deed was done, I put my knife away, took the light from him and shined it down the road.

The world was silent. No crickets chirped in the weeds this time of year. No breeze sighed through the trees. The road stretched out before us beneath the flashlight's beam as if we were staring into a tunnel that continued into forever.

"Let's move," I said.

We started walking.

Gravel crunched beneath our shoes. I craned my head toward the heavens as we walked. A waning gibbous moon peered down at us like the heavy-lidded eye of someone fighting sleep, perhaps a drunkard whose son had spiked his beer with 3-2-1-ZZZ's. That thought made me chuckle uneasily. Matthew asked me what was funny, and I told him it was nothing. An owl hooted. It sent chills up my spine, sounded like a human voice trying to mimic the nightbird's call. I imagined a trio of bullies hiding in the woods, preparing to ambush my brother and me.

"What was that?" Matthew said.

"Just an owl."

"You're sure?"

"Relax. It's nothing to worry about."

But with every passing minute, I realized my bravery was a lie. I suddenly felt like I was three or four years old again–a toddler terrified of the dark–as I recognized the gravity of our situation for the first time. I stopped walking, glanced back toward the cabin. The lights in its windows resembled the pinprick eyes of some nocturnal creature stalking us from afar. A wisp of smoke snaked from the chimney. I thought of Dad inside, wondered if he was smiling in his sleep as he dreamed about drawing a bead on the buck. God, he was gonna be so pissed when he woke up…

I shined the light in Matthew's face. He winced and looked away. I noticed his teeth were chattering. Mine were too.

"Maybe we should wait until morning," I said. "It's really cold out here."

"I'm freezing," Matthew said. "But what about Dad?"

"Between the beer and the pills, I'm pretty sure he'll be out most of the night. We'll start walking around dawn, when it's a little warmer."

"Okay," Matthew said. "If you're sure."

I *wasn't* sure. I thought of my favorite story in the Bible, the one about Daniel in the lions' den. God had protected him from harm, but Daniel wasn't dumb enough to go back inside after he survived the night. That would have been downright foolish.

I wished I had thought this whole thing through a little better. But I could never admit to my little brother that I was just as scared as he was.

"You gotta be quiet," I whispered, as we crept up the steps to the porch. "Don't make a sound."

"Okay," he said.

"I mean it, Matthew. Don't even *breathe*."

I killed the flashlight. As I eased open the screen door its creak was louder than Gabriel's trumpet on Judgment Day.

We tiptoed to the couch that sat about six feet behind Dad's chair. Draped over the back was an old wool blanket. Matthew and I each took an end of the couch and got beneath the blanket, trying to make ourselves comfortable.

I glanced over at the clock on the wall by the woodstove. It was a quarter past nine. We had a long way to go until morning.

My brother drifted off to sleep a few minutes later with his thumb in his mouth.

I clutched the hilt of my knife, watched Dad snore, and waited for the sun to rise.

PART TWO

CHAPTER FIFTEEN

This is the point in my story where there are parts that I can't promise are a hundred percent accurate. A lot of it occurred somewhere else, while my brother and I were putting our plan into motion. I'm filling in the gaps the best I can, based on what I heard from the police and saw on the news afterward. Some of what was said between certain parties might have been slightly different from the way it really happened...

...so if I flub a few of the minor details, forgive me. Most of the folks who would argue with me died that day, out there in the woods, so you won't hear them complain.

Beneath the first rays of dawn, Robert Caldwell set the last armload of gear—a pair of binoculars, a Coleman lantern, and two canvas rifle bags—into the back of his mud-spattered Wrangler and slammed the door. He was dressed in full camo without a hint of hunter's orange, because that was the only way to hunt.

He spat a gob of tobacco juice onto the ground before climbing into the Jeep.

His son waited in the passenger seat. He was also dressed in full camo. A large bandage covered Caleb's left temple.

"Ready?" asked the elder Caldwell.

"Ready," the boy replied, although he didn't look so sure.

"It'll be okay, son. This is the way men used to settle their scores. Old-fashioned frontier justice."

Caldwell backed the car out of their driveway then and sped off, ignoring the 15 MPH SPEED LIMIT signs posted throughout the trailer park.

In the doublewide across the road from the Caldwells' place, the blinds in one window snapped shut.

For once, Walt Gorman wasn't paying any attention to *Good Morning America* on the TV a few feet away. He turned from the window and barked at his son, "You better not be shitting me, Zack."

"I'm not," the teenager assured him. "Caleb talks to Becky Bullard sometimes, mostly trying to get in her pants. Her dad owns Liberty Guns & Ammo? Becky told Caleb that Mr. Bradersen was in the store a few days ago. Said he was bragging about taking his oldest boy out to Steck's Mill soon as deer season opens. He's got a cabin up there. Caleb says his dad knows where it's at 'cause him and Mr. Bradersen used to be close when they were kids."

"Get me the phone," said Walt. "Ain't no telling what Bob Caldwell's planning. That guy's got a crazy streak a mile wide."

Sheriff McLelland sat at her desk, finishing up some paperwork while she hummed along with the Fleetwood Mac song that was playing on the radio on the bookshelf behind her. She had been at it since five a.m., after conceding to her insomnia.

She put her pen down. Glanced at her watch. Rubbed at her temples and stared at a framed photo of her husband Donnie and their two children. She took a sip of black coffee from her travel mug with the Michigan State Spartans logo on the side, then picked up her pen again.

The phone rang.

"Can you take a message for me, Trudy?" McLelland hollered through the open doorway. "I'm busy."

"It's Walt Gorman," the dispatch officer replied from the next room. "His son is one of Caleb Caldwell's buddies. Says he's got something you need to hear, Sheriff."

McLelland picked up the phone.

CHAPTER SIXTEEN

A few minutes past seven a.m., our father woke up.

He grunted, tried to stand up, but realized his arms and legs were bound to his chair.

He growled like a wild animal from behind his duct tape gag, began to struggle violently. His sweaty hair flopped about. The chair's legs thumped on the cabin's hardwood floor. But after a minute or so he gave up. He sat there, moaning and breathing heavily through his nose.

I looked over at my brother. His hands covered his mouth. He was wide-eyed and trembling. I held a finger to my lips: *Shhh*. I nodded toward the kitchen area and mouthed the words: *Back door*.

Slowly, we climbed off of the couch.

Halfway to our destination, Matthew kicked the bottle cap that I had failed to dispose of properly after I had drugged Dad's beer with the sleeping pills. It clattered across the kitchen floor.

We froze. Matthew grabbed my arm.

Dad sat up straight. Twisted his head around in our direction. He rocked back and forth, from left to right, slamming his feet onto the floor until he had jostled his chair into a position where he could see us. He called our names from behind the duct tape, pleading with us to untie him.

We turned to face him.

I saw it in his eyes a moment later. He realized what had happened here.

He began to berate us. I couldn't understand all of the things he promised he would do to us if we didn't obey him, but I didn't have to.

"He's really mad," said Matthew.

"Kinda what I expected, squirt," I said.

And then…

I couldn't stop myself. I crossed the room, planted one foot in Dad's burly chest, and shoved with all my strength.

His chair tipped backward. He crashed to the floor with a muffled roar.

I grabbed Matthew's hand and we fled from the cabin as his muffled curses faded into the distance behind us.

CHAPTER SEVENTEEN

"Trudy," said the sheriff, "do you copy?"

A squawk of static on her radio, then: "Ten-Four, Sheriff. Whatcha need?"

"I'm seriously out of my jurisdiction here. Any luck reaching the sheriff in Steck's Mill?"

"He's at a training session in Morganville. Guy I talked to said he's indisposed 'til Sunday evening."

"And the State Police?"

"Busy at the border," the dispatcher replied. "Most of their resources are tied up dealing with the manhunt for that escaped convict."

"Wonderful. What about the map to Bradersen's cabin? Did you get that for me?"

"Sent it through a second ago, Sheriff."

McLelland clicked some keys on her laptop, pulled up a satellite image of the Bradersen property. An eighteen-wheeler rumbled by on the highway, close enough to rock her patrol car, which was parked on the shoulder beneath a Burger King billboard.

"You're a godsend, Trudy."

"I know," said Trudy. "I really deserve a raise."

"I agree," said the sheriff. "Remind me I said that when all of this is over."

"Count on it," Trudy said.

"McLelland, over and out."

She pulled into the flow of traffic and headed toward Steck's Mill.

CHAPTER EIGHTEEN

"You're crazy!" Matthew said as we ran, his breath pluming out of him in puffy white clouds. "I can't believe you did that!"

"Neither can I," I said.

"Are you sure he won't come after us?"

"We'd better hope he doesn't, after what we did."

"*We?*"

"Keep moving," I said. "It's a long way back to the main highway."

Our energy ran out a few minutes later. Our run slowed to a walk.

"Jake," Matthew said, "I don't know about this. What if we go back and apologize?"

I stopped walking. Stared at my brother.

Birds chirped in the treetops, as if eavesdropping on our conversation and adding commentary of their own.

He said, "We could tell him we made a big mistake and maybe he'll just—"

"You're kidding, right?" I said. "You think that'll be enough? After what we did to him, you'll say you're sorry and he'll just forgive you?"

Matthew shrugged, started sucking his thumb.

"No," I said. "I'll tell you what he'll do. He'll beat the crap out of you, just like he always does. And maybe…maybe he'll kill you this time."

"Please don't yell at me," he said.

"I'm not yelling at you. I'm just telling you like it is."

He thought about that for a moment, then said, "I don't really want to go back."

"Yeah, that's what I thought."

We came to a fork in the road.

"Which way?" Matthew asked me.

"This way," I said. "I think."

I changed my mind a few seconds later, and we headed in the other direction. Gravel turned to hard red dirt beneath our feet.

CHAPTER NINETEEN

Sheriff McLelland checked her map and slowed the patrol car as she turned onto a rutted dirt road. A chain lay to one side of the road, along with a muddy "PRIVATE PROPERTY/NO TRESPASSING" sign. It didn't take a diploma from the academy to deduce that the chain had been snipped with bolt-cutters.

She arrived at the cabin ten minutes later. She brought the patrol car to a smooth stop next to Dad's pickup, instantly noticed that the truck's tires were flat. She scanned her surroundings before climbing out of her vehicle and approaching the cabin with one hand on the holster of her gun.

She knocked.

Struggling noises from inside. The sound of muffled shouting.

McLelland drew her sidearm. Pressed her back against the wall and leaned over to peer through the window.

She saw Dad inside, tied to the tipped-over chair. They made eye contact. He screamed at her from behind his duct tape gag.

"Mr. Bradersen! I need to know if there's anyone else inside the cabin with you!"

Dad shook his head.

McLelland entered, swept the room with her Glock 22. She squatted down beside Dad, grabbed a corner of the tape and ripped it off his mouth.

"Gahh! That hurt!"

"Are you injured, Mr. Bradersen?"

"I don't think so. No, I'm okay. Jesus."

The sheriff pulled a buck knife from inside her jacket, started sawing at the coils of rope that bound him to the chair. "Did the Caldwells do this to you?"

"No." Dad's face burned bright red. "It was Jake and Matthew."

"I don't understand. Did you say your *sons* did th–"

"Yeah. Wait. What do the Caldwells have to do with this?"

"Mr. Bradersen, where are your boys now?"

"I don't know. I think they might be trying to run away."

"When did you last see them?"

"Half-hour, maybe? You wanna tell me what the hell's going on? You mentioned the Caldwells. Why would you bring up the Caldwells?"

"I got a call from Walt Gorman," McLelland explained as she finished cutting the last of the ropes. "His son is friends with Caleb Caldwell. He said Jacob was the one who attacked Caleb. He knew you and your boys were up here, and they're coming after you."

"What are you...coming after m–"

"I think they're planning to make it look like a hunting accident."

The sheriff tried to help Dad rise to his feet. He shrugged her off.

"Let him come! I see that son-of-a-bitch within a foot of my property, I'll blow his head off!"

The sheriff cleared her throat. "I'm not sure I'm the person you should be saying that to, sir."

"Come on, we'll take my truck," Dad said.

"Afraid not," said the sheriff. "Unless you plan to roll out of here on four flat tires."

Dad punched at the air. "Those little *bastards!*"

"It's fine. We'll take my patrol car."

"The boys don't know their way out," said Dad. "Probably scared shitless on top of that. Likely took a wrong turn or two. Patrol car will never make it on some of these back roads. We'll have to walk."

"Fine," McLelland said. "We'll walk."

Dad started rummaging through his hunting gear. "Lemme get my rifle first."

"I really wish you wouldn't," said the sheriff.

"Well, it's like my daddy used to say...wish in one hand, shit in the other, and see which fills up first."

CHAPTER TWENTY

The Caldwells came to the first fork in the road.

"We'll walk from here," Bob Caldwell told his son, as he pulled over and killed the ignition. "Keep the element of surprise. He'll never know what hit him."

Caleb gnawed at his fingernails.

His father got out of the Jeep. "Move your ass, boy!"

Caleb obeyed.

The older man opened the back door, unzipped the two canvas bags and removed from each a black semi-automatic assault rifle with a 30-round clip.

"This sure brings back memories. Used to come up here all the time with Kurt Bradersen and his daddy when we was in high school. A lot's changed since then. Blood's thicker than water and all that."

Caleb was silent.

Caldwell gave one of the guns to his son, kept the other for himself. The latter he had rigged "jungle-style," with a second clip of ammo turned upside-down and ready to go, secured to its partner via duct tape.

They started hiking for the cabin as morning birdsong filled the air.

CHAPTER TWENTY-ONE

I stepped in a dip in the road where it had been partially washed out by the rain, tripped and nearly went down. A flurry of crows burst from the woods and blackened the grey autumn sky, cawing angrily.

With every passing minute, I was more convinced that we had made a wrong turn. I couldn't tell Matthew. But he knew me better than anyone.

"You okay?" he asked. "What's wrong?"

"Just tired," I said.

"How much further, you think?"

"I don't know."

We walked on for another five or ten minutes. Then...

"Hey," I said. "Look at that."

It was a 1974 Chevelle Malibu. It had been there for so long the vehicle and nature had become one. It was surrounded by brush and dead tree limbs. Thick brown vines wrapped around it like a multitude of snakes slithering up from beneath the soil to choke the life out of a much larger animal. A crack shaped like an upside-down lightning bolt bisected its dirty rear window. Its tires were flat, the rubber rotted. Rust had eaten away most of its original pine-green paint job. GOD BLESS AMERICA, read the faded sticker on its bumper.

"What is it?" Matthew asked.

"It's a car," I said.

"I can see it's a *car,* smart-aleck."

I ignored him. Goosebumps prickled my forearms, and it wasn't because of the cold.

Something about that car...why did it look so *familiar?*

I stepped into the tall brown weeds that engulfed the vehicle and crouched down next to the driver-side door. I ran my fingertips along the punctured metal. My heart raced.

"That's a bullet hole."

"Whoa," said Matthew. "These too?"

He stood by the quarter panel. Three more small, round holes polka-dotted the rear wheel well.

"You think maybe this car belonged to some bank robbers?" Matthew exclaimed.

I shook my head.

"I do. I think that's what happened! Nobody ever found their getaway car, until we came along. Maybe there's a whole bunch of money inside!"

"If there was, do you think it would still be in there?" I said, although I was barely listening to my brother.

I spat on a window, rubbed some of the grime away. Cupped my hand to the glass and peered inside.

The car's interior was draped with thousands of silvery spider webs. On the backseat sat an old teal suitcase and a red raincoat.

I tried to swallow, but my throat was suddenly very dry.

"Jake, what's wrong?" Matthew pushed past me, stared through the window. "Spiders. I should have known. Scaredy-cat."

I shook my head again. Tried to think. Couldn't focus with Matthew rambling on about how the suitcase might have a million dollars in it. The pieces of the puzzle were there, but I didn't have the picture on a box to help me put them all together. I fumbled with the door handle. It was locked. I stared again, mesmerized, at those holes in the quarter panel. I rounded the back of the car, discovered at least half a dozen more bullet holes stippling the lid of the trunk.

"Jake! This side's open!"

The shrieking hinges of the passenger-side door startled me from my reverie. I stumbled around to that side, slammed the door before he got it halfway open, and pushed Matthew away from the car.

"No!" I said. "Don't."

"Why not? Whoever it belongs to isn't coming back. Obviously."

"Matthew," I said, with a tremor in my voice. "I want you...I want you to go stand over there."

"So you can open it? Forget it. I wanna see what's in there."

"Do what I tell you, Matthew. I'm not playing around. Do it now."

"You're not the boss of me."

"Don't make me hurt you, squirt."

"Okay!" He stomped away, stood with his hands on his hips in a spot no further from me than the distance between our beds back home. "Is this far enough?"

"No." I pointed toward a fallen tree about twenty feet away from the front of the car. "I want you to go stand by that tree."

"This ain't fair," he whined.

"Good boy," I said. "Now…turn around. Face the other way."

"What for? Am I in trouble for something?"

"No. You're not in trouble. Just do what I say, okay?"

He crossed his arms in front of his chest, pouting. He had never looked as small as he did at that moment, and I had never felt so protective of him.

I reached down, picked up a rock about half the size of a football. Mentally counted to three. Then I rammed the pointed end of the rock into the keyhole of the trunk's lid as hard as I could. The sound of my assault echoed through the forest: BAM!

Matthew flinched, turned around. "What in the world are you doing?"

"Tell you in a minute. Just stay where you are. Keep your back to me, no matter what."

"I can't see anything from over here anyway, Jacob. Why can't you tell me what's going on?"

I hit the keyhole again: BAM!

Again. "Because—" BAM! "—I hope I'm wrong."

"Wrong about what? You're not making any sense."

By now, I was out of breath. Sweat trickled down my forehead, into my eyes.

I gnashed my teeth and growled, "Come on…"

A flurry of blows then, desperate but growing weaker one by one: BAM! BAM! BAM…BAM…BAM.

Finally, the trunk popped open…and I screamed when I saw what was inside.

A skeleton. It had once been a woman, judging from what was left of her faded pink dress. A few wisps of matted brown hair still clung to the yellowed skull. Her knees were tucked into her body, her hands folded at her chest. She seemed to grin up at me. Silver glistened in the back of her mouth, where she had a cavity filled. Her smell wafted up into my nostrils, but she had been here for so long it was not an odor of decay. She smelled of mildew and dust. Like our storage shed back home.

I dropped the rock. Staggered back from the car. My butt struck the cold, hard ground.

Matthew ran toward me. "Jake, what is it? Are you okay?"

I scrambled to my feet, slammed the lid of the trunk down, and blocked my brother from coming any closer.

"Is it the bank robber's body?"

I gripped him by the shoulders. Shook my head back and forth, back and forth.

"What is it, then?"

"It's nothing."

"I never heard you scream like that. People don't scream over nothing. Let me *see!*"

"No."

"Whatever it is, I can take it. Stop treating me like I'm a baby."

"I can't...I can't let you see what's in there, Matthew."

"Get out of my *way!*"

He shoved me. Any other time, my brother could have never overpowered me. But I was out of breath, weak from my assault upon the trunk lid and in shock from what I had seen. I went down again...

...and the lid of the trunk slowly rose.

Matthew approached the rear of the car.

"Matthew," I cried, "please don't..."

"Jacob? Matthew? Is that you?" a voice echoed through the forest then.

"Oh, God," I said. "It's Dad!"

"I've got the police with me!" Dad called out to us. "You two are in a lot of trouble, you hear me?"

"What do we do?" Matthew asked me.

"This way!"

I ran for the fallen tree. He followed me. We lay flat on our bellies behind it just as our father and Sheriff McLelland appeared at a curve in the road perhaps fifty yards away. Dad led the way with his hunting rifle.

Matthew's wide eyes pleaded with me to get us out of here. I held a finger to my lips, shook my head. He slapped a hand over his mouth, nodded.

"You don't need to run anymore, boys!" This time it was the sheriff speaking. "I know about what happened with Caleb, and I believe it was self-defense on your part, Jacob. I need you to show yourselves so we can work this out. I want to help you."

Against my better judgment I yelled back at them, "This isn't about Caleb Caldwell!"

Matthew pinched my arm. His expression scolded me: *What are you doing? You said we gotta be quiet!*

We peeked over the tree trunk, watched as Sheriff McLelland and our father paced from one side of the road to the other, trying to determine where my voice had come from. Less than fifty feet away from them sat the old car and the horror hidden inside of it.

"Wanna tell me what it's about, then?" the sheriff shouted back at me.

"This is about our dad," I replied.

I saw Dad grip his rifle tighter.

McLelland glanced back at him. "What's that mean?"

Dad shrugged. "I dunno."

"Tell him to put his gun down!" I said.

Their heads turned in our direction. My heart skipped a beat. For a moment, I was sure that they had looked right at us.

"I don't know what's gotten into you boys," Dad said, "but if you don't come out right this second, you're gonna be grounded 'til you're thirty."

"Let's keep this friendly," said the sheriff. "Put your gun down, please, Mr. Bradersen?"

He gave her a look that suggested he couldn't believe a woman had the nerve to try telling him what to do, but then did as she asked. He set his gun down, butt on the ground, its barrel against a birch tree.

"Now, you heard the lady sheriff," he said. "You boys show yourselves."

"Everything's gonna be okay," said McLelland.

"You see that car?" I hollered back.

"I see it," the sheriff said.

"Open the trunk."

I saw Dad go tense from head to toe. He started chewing at his bottom lip.

"What am I gonna find in there?" the sheriff asked me.

"I don't want to say in front of my brother."

"Why not?" Matthew whispered. "What is it?"

I wiped tears from my eyes with my shirt sleeve, shook my head before shouting back at the sheriff, "Open it! You'll see!"

Sheriff McLelland approached the car with one hand on her hip.

Dad picked up his rifle, brought the stock to his shoulder.

Before I could warn her, he aimed it at the back of the sheriff's head and pulled the trigger.

Her face exploded in a crimson cloud. She fell forward into the dirt.

The gunshot echoed throughout the forest along with our screams.

"See what you made me do?" Dad roared to the sky, as he loaded another round into the chamber.

He brought the rifle to his shoulder and led with the barrel, pointing it toward our hiding place.

I grabbed Matthew's hand, and we took off into the deepest part of the forest.

Limbs lashed at our face and arms. Briars slashed at our clothes.

"I'm scared, Jake," Matthew cried. "He's gonna kill us, ain't he? Our own dad's gonna kill us!"

"Just keep moving and try not to think about it!"

"Why did Dad kill the sheriff?"

"Because. That was Mom's car back there. That was her stuff in the backseat."

"What are you talking about?"

"It wasn't a bank robber's body in the trunk. It was Mom's."

His jaw dropped.

"I think she was trying to leave him. She probably planned to come back for us, I don't know. But she tried to leave and I think Dad killed her and all this time he's been saying she abandoned us."

"I don't want to die!" my brother wailed.

"Neither do I. We gotta find our way back to the cabin. Follow me. Keep up."

Dad rummaged through the sheriff's pockets until he found her keys. He tried not to look at her face as he did so—it was a hideous red crater that barely resembled anything that had once been human.

He grabbed her legs, started dragging her toward the old car. The Malibu had been Dad's first set of wheels when he was a teenager. He was driving it the night he met Mom at our favorite restaurant.

"Gonna have to move over, Jeanette," he said between labored breaths, "share some space with Dickless Tracy."

He dropped the sheriff's body, swept the rock off the lid of the trunk. The lid creaked open. He didn't look down at the skeleton inside. Moving quickly, he hefted McLelland's corpse in a fireman's carry, and dumped her on top of Mom.

He closed the lid, but it popped back open. He picked up the rock, closed the trunk again, then set the rock on top and headed back for his rifle.

Suddenly, a gunshot kicked up the dirt just a few inches from Dad's foot. He yelped, jumped back.

"Not another move and I mean it!" someone shouted.

"Who the fuck is that?" said Dad.

"Surprise," Bob Caldwell said, as he and his son stepped out from behind a tree, their guns pointed at Dad.

"You're trespassing, you piece of shit," Dad said.

"Don't think the law will care much too much trespassing when they hear about you killing one of their own," Caldwell said.

"Who's gonna tell 'em?"

"You're looking at him."

"You gotta get out of these woods alive before you can run your mouth," said Dad.

"I figure I'll manage," said Caldwell.

He took careful aim at Dad's left ear and pulled the trigger. The shot was dead-on. The bullet ripped off his earlobe.

Dad shrieked, slapped his hand to the wound.

Caldwell roared with laughter, punched his son on the arm. Caleb offered his father a weak smile.

"Son of a bitch!" Dad said. "What the hell did you do that for?"

"So you don't forget who's in charge here," Caldwell said.

Dad glared at him. Blood ran through his fingers and trickled down his forearm.

"To your cabin, Kurt," said Caldwell. "Best you get to walkin'."

My brother and I sprinted across the clearing to the sheriff's patrol car.

Its doors were locked.

"Dammit!"

"I could get a hammer out of Dad's toolbox," Matthew said.

"Do that," I said. "Great idea, squirt!"

When he handed the hammer to me, I wrapped both hands around its handle and hit the driver-side window. It bounced off. I did it again. The glass refused to crack.

"Come on." I threw the hammer to the ground and ran to the cabin with Matthew in tow.

As soon as we were inside, I pulled a chair up next to the gun rack. The pink eyes of the albino buck in the nearby photograph stared into my soul as I hefted the rifle and carefully stepped down with it. I thought about what Dad had said in the past, about how the old gun might not even fire anymore. But I could see no other option. For that matter, would I remember everything he had taught me about marksmanship through the years when it counted? I had to try and hope for the best.

I ran to the kitchen, threw open the drawer where I had found the duct tape the night before. I remembered seeing a box of ammo in there.

"Oh, God," Matthew said. "Jake, you should come here and look at this!"

"I'm busy, squirt. What is it?"

"The Caldwells. They've got Dad."

I ran to the window and watched with him.

"Holy shit..."

"Yeah," Matthew said. "Holy shit."

"Saw you take her keys," Caldwell said. "Give 'em to me, asshole."

Dad reached into his jacket, gave them up.

Caldwell tossed the keys to his son. "Caleb, unlock the car. Should be a radio inside."

Caleb unlocked the driver-side door of the sheriff's patrol car, leaned into the vehicle, and came out with a walkie-talkie.

"Hold on to that," Caldwell said. "You're gonna call it in and tell them what he did. But first, I wanna have a little fun. Go in there and get me a couple of beers."

Dad's features hardened.

Bob Caldwell smiled. "That's right, shithead. It's payback time." He turned to his son. "What are you waiting for, boy?"

Caleb laid his rifle on the hood of the patrol car, shoved the walkie-talkie inside his jacket, and ran for the cabin.

"Hide!" I told Matthew. "Quick!"

I opened a pantry door and shoved my brother inside. I crammed in behind him and closed the door behind us just as Caleb stormed into the cabin.

I heard him open the refrigerator. Bottles clinked together.

The screen door slammed as Caleb went back outside.

Matthew and I burst out of the pantry and ran back to the window.

Keeping his gun aimed with his right hand, Caldwell took a bottle in his left and guzzled loudly. Some of it ran down his chin but he didn't wipe it away. He threw the bottle into the woods, motioned for the next one. Caleb obliged him and he killed another beer just as quickly. This time he dropped the empty bottle onto the ground beside him.

"I'm all set now." He belched. "Go ahead and get on your knees."

My father scowled at him.

"On the ground now!" Caldwell shouted.

Dad did as he was told.

"That's a good dog. Now...hands behind your head."

Caldwell gave Caleb his gun. Unzipped his camo jacket.

Matthew looked up at me and whispered, "What's he doing?"

"I think...the same thing Dad did to him that night," I said. "After Caleb busted my nose and got blood all over his Army jacket."

Caldwell gave a little shake of his shoulders, as if trying to relax. And then he unleashed a yellow stream of urine, soaking Dad's chest and stomach. He tilted his head back and his laughter echoed through the clearing.

Caleb stood nearby, clutching the gun and staring off into the woods as if he was thinking about making a run for it.

"How's that feel, huh? Warming you up a bit?"

Caldwell gripped his penis in one hand and raised the stream.

When the piss hit his neck, Dad fought back.

He scissored his legs, and, with a roar, he knocked Caldwell off his feet. The smaller man hit the ground. Dad grabbed the beer bottle Caldwell had dropped, hurled it at Caleb. The bottle struck him in the thigh, didn't shatter, but caused Caleb to reflexively pull the trigger.

The shot hit Bob Caldwell in the face.

"No!" Caleb screamed.

Dad jumped to his feet, yanked the rifle away from Caleb.

Caleb threw his hands in the air. "P-Please don't shoot me, Mr. Bradersen. This was all my daddy's idea. I'm s-sorry. Please. I swear to God, I didn't want nothing to do with it."

"I oughta blow your fat head off," said Dad. "All these years, you've made my boy's life a living hell."

"I'm s-sorry," Caleb said again, squeezing his eyes shut as he waited to die. "Oh, God...D-Dad..."

"Suck it up," said Dad. "You'll live to bury your old man as long as you do exactly what I say."

"Y-Yes, sir. Anything..."

Dad nodded toward Caleb's rifle, lying on the hood of the patrol car. "First of all, take your gun and throw it in the woods. And don't try nothing funny."

Caleb's eyes slowly opened.

"Do it!"

Caleb did it.

"Now you're gonna use the radio to tell everyone it was your dad who killed the sheriff."

Caleb looked like he might vomit. But he nodded.

"What are you waiting for?" Dad said. "Make it sound convincing, boy."

With trembling hands, I loaded a round into the rifle's chamber: KA-CLACK!

Damn thing would probably blow up in your face if you tried, my father's voice taunted me in my head, *like everything else that's pretty on the outside....*

"He's gonna get away with it," I said. "He can't get away with it."

I closed one eye, brought the other to the scope and lined up my father's head in the crosshairs.

"Jake," Matthew said, "what are you–"

I pulled the trigger. The bullet whizzed past Dad's head, lifting his hair on that side. It shattered the rear window of the patrol car.

Dad dove for cover behind the car.

Caleb fled into the woods, crying and screaming with his hands covering his head. His pale butt-crack was the last thing I saw of him, disappearing into the darkness.

Matthew took his fingers out of his ears. "Did you get him?"

"You're gonna regret that, boy!" Dad bellowed.

I pulled the trigger again. This time my shot destroyed the taillight a few inches from Dad's head.

He dropped to the ground, started crawling across the gravel toward his truck.

"I swear to God, you're gonna regret that!"

He brought up Caldwell's gun, aimed toward the cabin and squeezed off five quick shots.

My brother and I hit the floor as the bullets burst through the walls, turned the chairs and kitchen table into splinters. Matthew screamed even louder than the chaos all around us.

I risked another glance over the windowsill, saw Dad peeking over the hood of the pickup.

I tried to fire off another shot but the Winchester jammed.

I thought about how he often boasted that you couldn't hide shit from your father 'cause fathers knew everything...as Dad made a dash for the cabin.

I shoved Matthew through the back door and we took off through the woods. Gunshots rang out behind us. The bark of a nearby tree exploded less than a foot from my head. We ducked. I jerked my brother sharply to the left as another gunshot ricocheted off a boulder, throwing sparks.

"What are we gonna do?" Matthew sobbed.

"We gotta circle around back toward the road but stay deep enough in the woods where he can't see us."

We ran.

Dad cursed beneath his breath as he staggered back outside, smelling of sweat and another man's piss.

He threw himself into the sheriff's patrol car. Cranked the engine. Stomped down on the gas pedal. The Lincoln's back tires sprayed up gravel like a boxer spitting up broken teeth as the vehicle careened across the clearing, back toward the main road that led out of here.

"Please," Matthew wheezed, "can we stop?"

"No. We have to keep moving."

"Stop, Jake. Please. I can't..."

"We have to keep moving, Matthew!"

"Can't we find a place to hide?"

I glanced around. Gasped when I saw a flash of white through the trees.

"Jake," Matthew said, "what's wrong?"

"Shut it!" I whispered, pointing.

With a rustle of leaves and a crack of twigs, it stepped into view then...

...the albino buck.

The photo in Dad's cabin did the beast no justice. I had never seen anything so beautiful, before or since. He was as white as newly-fallen snow, with haunting pink eyes like those of a pet bunny one of my classmates had brought to Show and Tell when I was in the second grade. His twelve-point antlers were the darkest part of him, the color of old chocolate. His haunches were sleek and muscular. As we stared at the buck and he stared back at us, he appeared to have no fear. He didn't snort. His tail did not perk up.

Slowly, he marched into the understory.

I motioned for Matthew to follow me.

The buck stepped into a scrape, a small cave made from bushes. He pawed at the ground several times, turning over the dead leaves and pine needles to get to the black soil beneath.

"What's he doing?" Matthew whispered.

"He's finishing his scrape."

"What's a scrape?"

I shushed him again.

And now the buck's tail did perk up. His nostrils flared as he heard something coming.

It was the sound of an engine revving. A vehicle, headed our way.

I started running again, pushing Matthew ahead of me.

"Get in," I said.

"What?"

"Get in the scrape. Go!"

The buck looked back at us. Its head twitched, its giant antlers wobbling oh-so-slightly.

It seemed to say: *Follow me.*

I let it lead the way.

I shuffled through the scrape, back bent, leading my brother by the hand. The smell of musky earth and animal pee filled my nostrils. Something chittered in the brush to my left, but I paid it no mind.

"What now?" said Matthew.

"Keep quiet. No matter what."

I fussed with the Winchester until I ejected the bullet that had jammed. Matthew picked it up, stuck it in his pocket. I loaded another one in the chamber, then aimed the rifle in what I thought was the direction of the road. Toward the sound of the oncoming car.

We waited for a few more minutes, then flinched when we heard Dad calling to us from the patrol's car speaker.

"Boys? Come on out now. Let's talk about this. You're in a lot of trouble, but we can make things right again. That's what family does. If you can hear me, I want you both to know how sorry I am."

I searched for the car through the rifle's scope.

"Can you see him?" Matthew asked me.

"Not really. Keep quiet."

"I think you got the wrong idea about some things," Dad's metallic voice echoed through the woods. "I want you to come out so we can talk about it."

"Jake?" said Matthew.

"I told you to be quiet."

"But I have an idea."

"What is it?" I said.

"What if I go out there?"

"You must be out of your mind."

"I think maybe I could…like…lure him out of the car."

I removed my eye from the scope and stared at my brother.

"Come on now, boys," Dad beckoned. "Show yourselves. I know we can work this out. Like we always do. Get things back on track."

"I think it'll work," said Matthew. "What other options do we have?"

Sometimes he could be wise beyond his years, when I allowed him to be.

I gave him a sad little smile, mussed up his hair. "Go. But be careful. I'll be right here, squirt. And if I get the shot…I'm gonna take it."

I saw his tiny Adam's apple twitch as he swallowed. "Okay."

"You hear me, boys?" Dad said on the speaker. "Everything can go back to the way it was."

Matthew crept along a deer path, through the bushes, heading in the direction of Dad's voice and the sound of tires rolling across dirt.

I crab-walked to the entrance of the scrape, keeping my brother in sight. I brought the rifle to my shoulder.

"Matthew!" said Dad. "Stop right there, young man!"

I spotted the patrol car through the trees.

Its brakes whined as it came to a stop. Dad got out. He lifted his hands into the air. "Matthew. Hey, buddy. Look...I don't have a gun. I just wanna hug you, son."

Matthew turned his back to Dad, facing toward me now.

I peered through the scope. Had a clean shot. But only for a second. Then Dad stepped forward and there was a giant oak tree in my way.

I sucked in a deep breath, let it out slowly. Wiped sweat from my brow with the back of one hand. Took another breath and held it.

"Please, Matthew," said Dad. "Get your brother and let's go home."

He took another step toward Matthew. Once again, I had a clean shot.

I thought about what I had seen in the trunk. About what he had done to our mother.

Squeeze the trigger, don't pull it...

I squeezed the trigger.

The bullet struck him in the right shoulder. He screamed, grabbed the wound.

I scrabbled for the box of ammo in my pocket. Dropped several bullets before I chambered another round. Aimed. Fired. Missed.

By now, Dad had retrieved Caldwell's rifle from the patrol car. He turned, started shooting wildly into the woods.

I ducked, covered my head, felt bullets whizzing by–tearing through leaves, ripping bark, and pinging off rocks.

Dad emptied the gun. He ripped the duct tape from around the "jungle-styled" clips, let the empty fall to the ground and jammed in the new one. The tape stuck to his hairy forearm, but, if he noticed, he didn't care. He peered into the woods, squinting, trying to find me this time instead of wasting ammo.

He shouted my name. His voice was hoarse.

I brought the scope to my eye. My hands were shaking violently. Couldn't hold the gun steady...

Dad stepped out of the road and into the woods, scowling.

And suddenly, through the scope, I saw Matthew crash into him at full speed. Dad lost his footing, went down.

I scrambled out of the scrape.

My brother swung his arms like a pinwheel, punching Dad in the side of the head, on his wounded ear. Dad warded off most of the blows, and after a few seconds, managed to push Matthew off of him.

"You little shit," he growled, as he rolled over and reached for the gun. "You are in so much trouble."

I stepped out of the woods and pointed the Winchester at him.

"Matthew, get the gun," I said.

Matthew rose to his feet. Walked around Dad, careful to keep out of his reach. He picked up the gun, eyeing it as if it were a venomous snake that would strike at any second.

"Careful, squirt. Bring it here."

"Don't do it, Matthew," said Dad. "Give it to me instead."

Matthew hesitated.

"Don't listen to him," I said. "I told you what he did to Mom."

"Matthew," said Dad. "Listen to me, son—"

"You know what he is," I said.

Dad said, "Give me the gun. Your brother's not your boss. I'm your father. Do what I say now, son."

Matthew glanced back and forth between our father and me.

Dad lunged for him.

My rifle spat a ball of fire and Dad's chest exploded. He took two faltering steps to one side, then collapsed in the dirt.

I ran to Matthew, and we stood over our father.

Dad coughed up bubbles of blood. A hideous gurgling sound came from inside of him.

He reached a trembling hand out toward us. We stepped back.

"I'm sorry," he said.

And then he was gone.

I threw down the rifle.

Heard something moving in the woods behind us.

I looked back. It was the albino buck, standing just beyond the tree line, about thirty feet away.

It watched us for a moment, before running off.

"Let's get out of here," I said.

I headed for the patrol car.

"I thought you couldn't drive," said Matthew.

"Pretty sure this one's an automatic. I'll figure it out."

"Maybe I can help you," he said.

"Maybe." I winked at him, and during that moment I felt more love for my little brother than I had ever felt before.

EPILOGUE

That night was the last time I saw Caleb Caldwell, the boy who had once been the scourge of my existence. It wasn't because he wandered off into the woods and was eventually eaten by wolves, although I might have wished such a fate would befall him once upon a time.

We had only travelled about a hundred feet down the road when he stumbled out of the woods, into our path. I slammed on the brakes, came within inches of turning my archenemy into a pancake.

Through the shattered window I told him he could get in the back.

As we drove on, he must have apologized a hundred times, swearing to God that he never meant for any of this to happen, until my brother said, "All right, already. You're giving me a headache."

A few minutes later, the night exploded with swirling red and blue lights, as our path was blocked by an army of patrol cars with STECK'S MILL POLICE DEPT on their side panels.

After his dad's funeral, I heard Caleb moved up north to live with his mom and his stepdad. I never saw him again.

Matthew and I became wards of the state, as Dad's only living relative was a great aunt who lived in a nursing home in Ohio. We grew up as well-adjusted as you would expect for two boys whose father had tried to murder them. We lived with several different foster families through the years, and although it was difficult the system was able to keep us together. I don't know how either of us would have survived, otherwise.

I dropped out of high school when I turned sixteen, but got my G.E.D. at the local community college. Eventually, I built a solid a career out of automotive repair, realizing I had a knack for it like my father and his father before him. I sold Dad's place–there's an RV dealership on the property these days–and I now own a chain of successful Top-Notch Auto

Repair shops in my hometown. Not long after I opened the first one, I married one of my customers. We were divorced a year later. I am currently involved with a lovely young lady named Brenda. She is pregnant with my first child, whose name will be Jacob Jr.

I read somewhere that a large percentage of boys, when asked what they would like to be when they grow up, say they want to be a fireman. My brother was no exception, especially after he saw all the coverage on TV about the heroes who worked at Ground Zero in the days following 9/11. Not long after his eighteenth birthday, Matthew (who now goes by "Matt") moved to New York City and got a job with the FDNY. These days we only get to see each other around the holidays, but when we do it's as if no time has passed at all. He still rings me up for advice now and then, and still calls me his big brother.

Matt has struggled with his demons through the years. I suppose it was inevitable that at least one us would inherit our father's addiction. He is in recovery, however, and doing well. The last time I spoke with him, he had just received his two-year sobriety chip.

Matt recently married his high-school sweetheart and they are expecting their first son as well.

He plans to name the boy Kurt. I have yet to ask him why. I suppose he has his reasons.

A month or so after what happened out there in the woods, I got rid of the rest of the comics stored in Grandpa's locker. I didn't sell them, though I'm sure Round Man would have been happy to take books without holes off my hands.

I boxed them up, and I had them delivered to Sheriff McLelland's kids.

It wouldn't bring their mother back, but Matthew and I figured they might enjoy them, and it was the least we could do.

One of my favorite writers once said that anybody who has survived his childhood has enough information about life to last him the rest of his days. I didn't understand what that meant when I was a young. Now I understand completely.

The world is a scary place for a kid. It's even scarier when you're forced to watch your back because those who are supposed to protect you are those you should fear the most.

But life is good, more than it's not. I believe that. And I will do everything I can to make sure that my son believes it too. I cannot wait to give him everything that our father neglected to give my brother and me.

Perhaps one day I will take Jake Jr. on his own hunting trip. Perhaps little Kurt can come with us.

And maybe, just maybe, the albino buck will still be out there.

ABOUT THE AUTHORS

James Newman is the author of numerous works of horror and suspense, including the novels *Midnight Rain*, *The Wicked*, *Animosity*, and *Ugly as Sin*, and the collections *People Are Strange* and *The Long N' Short of It*. *In the Scrape* is his most recent collaboration, following fan favorites such as *Dog Days O' Summer* (co-written with Mark Allan Gunnells), *Scapegoat* (with Adam Howe), and *The Special* (also with Mark Steensland, and soon to be a major motion picture!).

Mark Steensland self-published his first book while in fourth grade, and has been telling stories ever since--some of them true. He became a professional journalist at the age of 18, writing about movies for such magazines as *Prevue* and *American Cinematographer*. His award-winning films have played in festivals around the world. His novel for young readers, *Behind the Bookcase*, was published in 2012. His novel for adults, *The Special*, was published in late 2018 and is now being made into a feature film. He currently lives in California with his wife and their three children.

Printed in Great Britain
by Amazon